Th

A PARANORMAL SHIFTER ROMANCE

JASMINE WHITE

Get Yourself a FREE Bestselling Paranormal Romance Book!

Join the "**Simply Shifters**" Mailing list today and gain access to an exclusive **FREE** classic Paranormal Shifter Romance book by one of our bestselling authors along with many others more to come. You will also be kept up to date on the best book deals in the future on the hottest new Paranormal Romances. We are the HOME of Paranormal Romance after all!

*** Get FREE Shifter Romance Books For Your Kindle & Other Cool giveaways**

*** Discover Exclusive Deals & Discounts Before Anyone Else!**

*** Be The FIRST To Know about Hot New Releases From Your Favorite Authors**

Click The Link Below To Access Get All This Now!

SimplyShifters.com

Already subscribed?
OK, *Turn The Page!*

About This Book

When Nika signed up to what she thought was a normal dating website she just wanted a bit of excitement in her life.

However, she had no idea what she was about to let herself in for. It turns out the dating site that Nika has joined is mainly for shifters who want to find a mate.

So when Nika meets the hot and sexy Nathan from the same site she is excited to meet him and find out more about her potential date.

Little does she know, Nathan is in the running to become the **NEXT ALPHA** of his pack and so he does not see her as a potential date but as a potential **MATE** and someone he needs to help him gain his alpha status.

Has Nika bitten off more then she can chew? Or is she willing to embrace the shifter world in more ways than one?

CHAPTER ONE

Nathan lifted his snout to the air, testing the currents of wind that carried all the hidden scents and nuances of the wilderness before him. Even in his wolfish form he was able to appreciate the beauty of the rolling landscape. Thick spruce and fir forests clambered up the riven hillsides and mountains until it became too steep and gave way to sheer precipices of granite that shot straight up out of the earth like a giant's row of sharpened teeth. The image was hard to dispel. No doubt it was Clara who had first given him that metaphor.

The Giant's Jaw, he thought, his own human mind leaking through his animals' instincts. That was the name for the vast stretch of mountains that cut across the horizon, enclosing the glacial-cut valley below. He licked his lips and opened his mouth again, his own fangs glistening with saliva. He lifted his muzzle once more and tasted it; a faint trace of smoke, somewhere. Also spoor from the mountain goats that remained higher up, nestled among the crags that shadowed behind him.

He was not an overly impressive Wolf while in form, not like some of the other Alphas who were big around the shoulders and girth, as big in their human shapes as they were in their human ones. Rather, Nathan was more compact, as if everything about him had wrapped itself tightly into a firm package of fur and muscle. His dark grey pattern on his back and down his tail gave him a unique appearance though, one which made him look older than he actually was. It was for that reason, he figured, that the Alpha-hood of the pack had fallen on his shoulders.

Not yet, he reminded himself, taking a step back from the ledge. It wasn't official yet, Clara reminded, though it was she who had spent the last few months advocating her younger brother for the leadership role. Even against Nathan's firmest desires.

He seemed to shrug, and trotted back down the animal path that wended down through the clearing to the distant road below. The Trans-Canada highway when viewed from so high up was like a tiny grey filament of light smoke traversing the landscape, east to west. To the west, more mountains and dense forest, glaciers and the daunting peaks of the Canadian wilderness. To the east, Calgary and home. It was nearing evening, but there was still enough light to see by. Near a small river that hedged the highway he sniffed out the cache where he'd deposited his clothes and let his transformation back into a human follow its natural course.

Stooped over on all fours, his tail began to revert, and the hair sloughed off of him like dust, coating the ground around him like pine needles. He shook, trying to clear the cobwebs. It was always a bit disorienting when switching forms, and it took him several moments to stand up shakily. His naked torso and mid-riff were tanned and bent with the sort of musculature you'd find on a trained fighter. In truth, he had always thought of himself as a pacifist. It was another trait, he figured, that Clara had capitalized on when trying to campaign for him.

"Why can't you just leave well enough alone?" he asked to no one, and shivered.

His pulled on his trousers and heavy hiking boots and threw his thin cotton T-shirt and button-up plaid shirt over one strong and burgeoning shoulder. The muscles rippled with the effort, wiry and dense as bundled rope.

Crouching low, he peered across the river, making sure that there were no cars. It would be one thing to emerge on the road as a wolf, but it was still a bit odd for a half-naked man to come clambering out of the bushes. He smiled, wondering what sort of conclusions a tourist could draw from that.

With eager and tempered balance he found the fallen cedar tree across the creek that he had used to cross it and carefully walked across it, his boots holding on the slick bark. The water rushed under him, that blue glacial silt color that so evoked in him memory of his childhood, and how they'd often visit nearby Banff or Canmore, daring each other to jump in the frigid waters.

Near the side of the road at a pull off junction, with a few run down picnic tables and newish looking toilet facility, he put both shirts back on and scratched his head. His prematurely silver hair really did make him look older, but the fact his triangular shaped face and deep set jaw could only belong to someone younger, was a strange paradox of countenance for people who met him for the first time. He wondered what impression he gave on those individuals. He didn't think of himself as handsome, even though he was the embodiment of all those masculine qualities. His dark eyes, almost cobalt like a night sky, scanned the road west where the sun was starting to plummet. His brow seemed perpetually furrowed and rectangular, as if he were in a state of permanent wistfulness.

Hardly, he thought, *I'm barely twenty-five and if Clara is right about me, like she usually is, I'm too reckless to be Alpha.*

It was one of the reasons he had taken off early in the morning on his motorcycle, streaking across the flat prairie land that spanned between here and the distant blinking city lights of Calgary. He needed to clear his head, escape the politics and drama of the Pack.

As he got on his bike, a new Ducati X600, and strapped the black matte helmet over his shaggy silver hair he half dreaded returning to the Den. The bike roared and took off, and he ducked his head and let the wind whip past his ears, helping him forget about the impending confrontation he knew he would be facing when he got back.

By time he reached Calgary, and had swerved onto the bypass and made his way to the Den, it was already night and the streetlights had come on. The Den, a humorous moniker he suspected he had his father to blame for, was one of the bigger mansions in the suburb district and was perched on a small knoll that looked over the downtown core, but was far enough away to avoid the traffic and chaos. Nathan had always thought of it as a sort of sanctuary. The long timber frame building housed not just himself and Clara, but also a number of other resident Pack members, including his two cousins and his older uncle.

"Where the bloody hell have you been?" Clara asked when he came in.

Her hair, like his, was the result of a fickle crossing of genes, and the long silver braid down her back whipped against her lower back like a whip. She was only a year older than him, but sometimes she felt like a maternal substitute, and she could be fiery tempered at the best of times. Like Nathan, she had also acquired the lean and muscular frame of both their parents, and she wore it well. Her jeans clung tightly to her athletic thighs, and the heels of both cowboy boots under the denim cuffs clicked against the tiled floor.

"Had to clear my head, went for a ride," he said bluntly, trying not to make eye contact.

Though they were the same height, he felt himself shrinking against her gaze. "I've had the whole house looking for you. You can't just up and leave like this Nathan. Not now, not with so much at stake. Do you have any idea how hard I've been working trying to hold the Pack together?"

He did, and felt a bit ashamed, but tried not to let it

show. "I'm sorry, Clara. Really… I just… it's been getting to me lately. I needed *out*, y'know? I know it was selfish of me, but if I stayed here a second longer I was sure my brain was going to explode." He tried to retain some diplomatic air. "It won't happen again."

Clara's lips twisted as she glared at her brother, and her piercing blue eyes, a shade lighter than his, seemed to burrow into the deeper parts of him. He had never tried to lie to Clara – some part of him knew, he could never get away with it.

She sighed, finally, and leaned against one of the walls and crossed her arms. "I know how you feel, little brother," she said, softer, "don't think I don't – this has been tough on all of us. I like to think that it's just me, sometimes. I guess we're both selfish, in our own ways. But you have to understand what's at stake here."

"I do," he said solemnly and took a step toward her, putting a hand on her shoulder.

"I'm being overly worrisome, aren't I?" she asked. It was a rare moment of vulnerability and Nathan felt a lump grow in this throat, unsure of how to answer. "I'm not angry at you, Nathan. Not really. I was just… worried. I can't lose you too."

It felt like talons had gripped his heart and suddenly tightened and he tried to fight back the swell of nausea and emptiness that threatened to swallow him up. There was the faintest evidence of tears looming in the corner of Clara's eyes, and when he saw them she turned away quickly to keep him from seeing.

It seemed impossible to believe, still. Three months ago both of their parents had been killed. To say it out loud still held a certain power, like a taboo magic. Something that made the world seem surreal, *un*real. Perhaps it was the nature of their deaths that had caused such a stir in the Pack. Who could have ever imagined that both the Alpha and his mate would succumb to something as fickle and trivial as a car accident?

"You're not going to lose me," he said, and tugged on her shoulder again until she was forced to face him. She wiped quickly at her eyes, and tried to smile. "I'm right here, see?"

She nodded and wrapped her thick arms around his neck. He could smell her perfume, something that was sweet like lupines or wild flowers in spring. She was very warm, and he closed his eyes, enjoying the sensation of being held, and of holding her back. "Sorry for being an idiot," she said.

"You're not," he flashed a reciprocal grin. "So, while I was being irresponsible and you were dealing with all the things I should've been here to do, have you made any progress? What does the Pack plan to do?"

She shrugged, smirking at his nonchalant acknowledgment. "Right now it's split… between you and Dean, of course."

Dean was their first cousin, along with his twin sister Flores. Unlike Nathan, Dean looked like a real Alpha; he stood more than six feet tall and had arms like tree roots and a chest that bulged outward like an old fashioned stove. His short military-cut blond hair did little to conceal an egg-shaped head. He was a jocular kid, but prone to angry outbursts. He could probably best any of the candidates for leadership in physical competition, but he was not the brightest.

"Dean and me?" Nathan asked, surprised that the two of them had made it onto equal ground. Secretly, he had hoped one of the other relatives, a second cousin or uncle, any of the extended family that had converged on Calgary to witness the new leadership, would have been the favorite.

"Don't look so surprised," Clara teased, combing a lock of silver hair from her eyes and giving him a knowing look, as if she'd read his mind. "The elders have been impressed with some of the things you've accomplished."

"Like what? I would be torn apart in a competition."

"Brute physical strength is only one aspect of leadership, and nowadays it's far from the most important. You've got a good head on those shoulders, and you're sharp. Stop deprecating yourself," she said.

"Aye," he murmured.

She approached him and looked out the big ceiling to

floor windows that enclosed the kitchen and living room area. During the last three months this had become their main area in the vast mansion, with Dean and Flores inhabiting another corner, and other aunts, uncles, and warriors relegated to the other floors.

"You really do look like you could use a break," she said at last, and rubbed his shoulders. "You know, if you do become Alpha, you're going to be expected to take a mate, just like dad did. Have you thought about that?"

He tried to brush her off. "Ugh, don't you start on me too!"

Clara laughed and dug her nails into the broad muscle of his shoulder. "C'mon!" she said playfully. "You're a helluva a specimen. Any girl would be lucky to have you."

"Yeah right," he said doubtfully.

She pinched his ear and walked back out of the kitchen. "There you go again," she murmured, "you know I'm right, right? I'm never wrong… and certainly not about this either." She gave him a wink that made him nervous and departed to her own room with a small chuckle.

Well at least she's feeling better, he thought, and headed upstairs to his own room.

It was modest, and the ceiling slanted downward

toward windows that looked west toward the Rocky Mountains. He booted up his laptop and logged on, and wrinkled his brow. In all the clamor, excitement and turmoil that his parents' deaths had flung the Pack into, he hadn't really ever considered the fact that the Alpha was required to take a mate. He took off his shirt and rubbed at his naked torso, fingering the library of different scars that lined his youthful body, and let himself relive the memory that each had held.

His own training had been rough, and in many ways, he was surprised at how well both he and Clara had ended up. Keeping the secret of their birthright, resisting the urge to take form, and learning to adapt to a human world was not an easy task. In many ways, he felt as if he had a split personality, like he was living two lives. In that sense, he was glad for Clara, if only because she existed in *both*, and it helped to clarify what was real and what wasn't.

But a mate, he thought. He smiled and closed his eyes.

*

Nika watched the blue Camry pull out and head down the street from the top window of her room. She let out of a sigh of relief, and slumped down on the old foldaway couch while her roommate James worked away at something in the kitchen. She rubbed her temples, *just another headache*.

"I don't know how I let you talk me into this," she

said, trying to put scorn into her voice so that it would reach Charles. "Good riddance to him," she added.

"Was he really that bad?" James asked, popping his bald head around the corner. It was quite comical, almost like a disembodied head with a shiny scalp and almost nonexistent eyebrows gaping at her behind his thin framed glasses. "I thought you two would hit it off immediately. Charles is totally into art and stuff," he said, and disappeared.

For the past two weeks, James had been prodding her to go out on a date. *Just one, for me*, he urged. She knew he was just trying to look out for her. At almost twenty-six, she had only had one boyfriend in her less than illustrious romantic history, and he had been a university undergrad who ended up being more interested in completing his PhD than actually dating. *We were both interested in different things*, she reconciled.

Still, she knew she was missing out on a certain part of life. She had a great career, as one of directors of the prestigious Swanson Gallery downtown (who'd of thought that a BA in Art History would have landed her such a job?). But it wasn't until she had moved in with her gay and eccentric roommate James, self-professed Bohemian and connoisseur of the finer things in life, that she had realized how cloistered her life had been.

Something left over from my parents, she thought, and gazed out the window again. She had always been driven, motivated, and ambitious; her childhood had been one of extremes. Even though her parents were both dead now, she had mixed feelings about them. *Ambitious.* She had never thought of that adjective as anything other than positive. But now she was seeing how it had isolated her. Other than James, who did she really have to associate with? It had astounded her how huge James' circle of friends was. Every weekend it seemed he was attending events, or potlucks, or concerts, or inviting his group back to their small two bedroom cramped apartment overlooking the Calgary River.

"How come you don't bring people over?" he had asked once, and she had balked, not quite sure how to answer the question, only because she hadn't posed it to herself before.

In her way, she was jealous of him, that natural born charisma was something she lacked, though objectively she knew it was because she had never practiced it. Now, as she listened to him operating the blender in the kitchen, she wasn't sure if she would *ever* fit into the same sort of world he belonged to.

Still, this latest attempt at a date had been James' ongoing mission to trigger a semblance of a social life in her. *Except every guy he chooses is either boring, egotistical, or more gay than he is*, she thought with a bemused grin.

"What are you doing in there anyway?" she asked, pulling off her canvas jacket.

The blundering stopped and he came around the

corner holding two tall glasses full of a yellowish concoction. She smelled banana. And rum.

“I wasn’t a hundred percent you and Charles would really click either,” he said with a frown, “so I had some ingredients for a banana daiquiri waiting for you. Just in case. Drink up, sweetheart.”

She smiled and accepted it. Her long dark hair pooled at her shoulders and when it caught the streetlights from outside the smudged window, a trace of red seemed to glint off of it. She was hardly in a position to call herself beautiful, though she knew more than a few guys over the years had thought so. James’ phrase was *fucking hot*, but she wondered whether or not to trust him, since she’d heard him use the same words to describe handsome guys whenever they were out in public.

“You’re the best,” she said, tasting it, “ugh, seriously, James, what’s wrong with me?”

“Nothing’s wrong with you,” he crooned.

She held up her glass and drank. It was strong, but then James never made anything weak. “Yes, there is… I don’t know what. But you were right about me.”

“I like being right, totally feeds my ego,” he said, “but I don’t think so.”

“It’s true! This is the second date you’ve put me out on, and… they’re nice, really. All of them. And I’m not just saying that because they're your friends. It's just that there isn't that… I don't know… what to call it…"

"Spark?"

"Sure," she offered, and slumped her shoulders.

James put his arm around her shoulders. "That just means it takes more to ignite you," he replied. "That's not a bad thing. It means when you do find the right guy, well… fireworks."

"Yeah, I feel like exploding," she finished the daiquiri and leaned back, rubbing her cheeks, "maybe there's something to the theory that you're supposed to gain certain social skills early on. I spent all my time in books or in front of a laptop, ignoring people. I'm willing to conclude that I'm like an old dog… can't teach me new tricks."

"Hey, that's not true," he said. He touched his chin, and his eyes flitted behind his glasses. "You get along with me fine. And I know you've been hanging out with that other girl at the gallery… new friend, right?"

"Hardly, we're… just colleagues. I don't have any friends. It sounds weird to say out loud, but I've gone so long without needing any, that I don't even know how to make them anymore," she said. "I know it sounds like I'm whining, sorry. But you, it's different… you're not like the other guys…"

“You mean not looking to get in your pants.” He gave a wry grin.

“That,” she admitted, and shook her head with a smile, “and you’re not trying to show off. I get it, most guys… even if they’re the most honorable and kind and honest, they’re still putting on a show. A mask, like hiding behind their own emotions… or their own invented façade. I think I should just give up on guys… I don’t know how to talk to them.”

She leaned her head back again, and closed her eyes. Beside her, James finished his daiquiri, sipping it quietly, and put it back down on the table. Nika didn’t see him throw a glance at her, one that was bordering on uncertainty, as if he were trying to make up his mind. He cleared his throat and picked up the glasses, carrying them to the kitchen.

“You know,” he started to say and then there was only the sound of him filling up their glasses again. Nika opened one eye and glared at the kitchen. James only began a sentence with *you know* if he was scared of someone’s reaction.

“What?” she murmured miserably.

“Ah, just thinking,” he came back out, handed her a second daiquiri, “maybe I’m the wrong person to suggest a new social circle. Maybe you should take the initiative on your own.”

“I wonder how that would work,” she said, and tipped the glass toward her lips, staring over the rim at

James. “Why? What do you mean? You’re acting weird and mysterious… that always makes me nervous.”

James smiled. “You should try a new dating website. I just found it… it’s uh,” he tilted his head, wondering how to continue, or if he should, until Nika kicked him gently in the side with a socked foot, “ah, I’m going to regret this. Here.”

He reached in his jeans and pulled out a folded piece of paper and held it between two fingers above her head. She looked at it and reached for it flimsily like an exhausted cat until he pulled it away again. “What is it?”

James lowered it again. “A dating website,” he replied, and saw her flinch. “Yah, I know what you’re thinking but this is… well, not exactly your average dating website.” He dropped it and she caught it as it fell. “It’s uh… designed for unusual people.”

“Like me?” she asked and stuck out her tongue.

“More like… those who are tired of hiding behind masks.”

She opened the piece of paper. It was laminated now, she saw, and there was just a single website address on it, nothing else. Courier type font. *Probably a hipster thing*, she thought, and looked up at James to try and confirm her suspicions. He just shrugged and sat down and took a big quaff of his second daiquiri.

"That's not very specific," she said.

He swallowed and gave her a knowing look. "There's… a lot you don't know about the world, Nika. I'm not being pedantic when I say that, there are facets to your everyday existence that you have no context for."

"And you do?"

He shrugged in a compliant way and gave her another gentle smile as he adjusted his glasses. "Let's just say that I'm a dilettante when it comes to figuring out this thing called life… but in my attempt to, I've come across more than a few interesting things. Things that most people take for granted, or just plain don't see," his eyes darted again, pupils sleek and sharp as tiny koi. "That card may give you some insight."

"I think I'm tired of people. Guys especially," she said, but put the laminate card in her pocket.

James shrugged and stood up, made a mock gesture of stretching. "Well, it's up to you precious, I'm just a messenger. But I guarantee… whether or not you find Mr. Right by going to that website, it will *definitely* shake up your dreary existence. And you, lovely woman, *need* to be shaken."

Nika knew it wasn't meant to sound cruel, but she felt a bit of disdain as she watched him stagger to his bedroom, and it was only after she heard the door shut that she reached in her pocket to look at the card again. She read the website again. THERIO.CV.CA.

Weird name for a dating website, she thought.

In her own room she stripped off her shirt and skirt and suddenly caught her reflection in the mirror. She made a face and hugged her chest, emphasizing her cleavage, and laughed at the image. She had to admit, in spite of whatever her own thoughts were about her appearance, there was something sexy about her appeal; her muscular thighs and lean torso were milky white, but smooth. She rubbed her hand across her belly, turned in the mirror. Part of her regimen consisted of three Tae Kwon Do classes a week, plus three days of bouldering at the local rock climbing.

I suppose it's paying off, she mused. Another trait bequeathed by her parents. While they'd been alive, they'd insisted that she take so many extra-curricular classes that she had often found it hard to balance her academic life. *And no room at all for socializing*. She didn't like the idea of blaming them for her inability to make relationships, for her shyness, or for her social ineptness. It didn't seem right. Still, a lingering doubt always seemed to be there.

"I'm not that undesirable, am I?" she asked out loud to her reflection.

Nika sighed. Raised her middle finger. *Don't answer that*, she wanted to say.

After she'd slipped on her pajama bottoms she opened her laptop on her bed, and almost against her will, typed in the dating website. When she pressed enter, the screen suddenly changed to a badly rendered depiction of a forest scene at night with a full moon. There were several animals in a clearing, ranging from foxes to bears, and as she ran her cursor over them they would highlight. Humoring it, she clicked on the wolf.

"Right," she said, craning over and reading the first batch of questions to create her profile, "what have I got to lose?"

CHAPTER TWO

Nathan had been thinking hard about what Clara had said, about the need to show some initiative, even if he still held his own uncertainties about whether he was the right choice for leadership. When he woke up, he saw that there were several notifications on his iPhone. He scrolled through them sleepily, not recognizing the address or the content.

"Therio… what?" he shook his head and put the phone back down. He hated getting up in the mornings; it always felt as if he'd never gotten enough sleep.

By time he came downstairs, most of the family was already gone, although Aaron was up. The burly wolf of a man was well into his sixties, but to look at him you'd guess him older – he had the same lean and muscular torso of the rest of the male Pack members, and even as one of the elders he still retained an uncanny strength, both in terms of physical endurance and personality. He was huddled over a huge mug of coffee when Nathan entered the kitchen shirtless. Aaron had on his iconic plaid shirt unbuttoned over a black t-shirt, and a white grizzled growth of white beard was sparking out on his cheeks. His deeply lined face was testament to the many years he had spent as a trapper up north.

Hard as a granite edge, Clara had said once, describing their uncle. He was the only one of the Pack who had actually been born in the wild, and who had lived there most of his life. Even Nathan and Clara, though they often ventured into the wilderness, were fundamentally urbanites. Still, Aaron had never begrudged any of them for it. He understood the progression of time, the need to adapt.

He's the one who should really be leader, Nathan thought. *But no, they needed someone young.*

"Morning, pup," Aaron said, without looking in his direction.

"How'd you know it was me?" Nathan asked, and poured himself his own cup. It was strong, which meant Aaron had probably made this batch.

"You walk quietly," Aaron grumbled, "the others are louder than a locomotive in a thunderstorm. But you, you've got something of that wild instinct. To be invisible, until you want to be seen."

"High flattery, coming from you."

Aaron sipped and scratched his cheeks. "Maybe. That reminds me, Clara was quite worried about you last night. You head to the Great Jaw?"

"How'd you know that?" Nathan raised an eyebrow.

"Just a hunch. You're like me, Nathan. Sometimes you just need to run. And there's only one place that really calls to our kind. To our pack, in particular," he sniffed. "How are you holding up?"

Nathan sighed. "You know how it is. Politics."

“Aye,” he muttered sympathetically.

Just then, Clara entered into the kitchen, putting on a tight leather jacket as she rushed to put bread in the toaster. She rapped Nathan on the top of the head. “You’re up early,” she said, “for you. The others have already left I take it? Morning, Aaron.”

“Mornin’ Clara,” the old wolf muttered, and gazed out the window.

She poured herself a cup of coffee as well, smelled it, and made a face before setting it back down on the counter. Nathan’s phone vibrated in the pocket of his cargo pants and he fished for it, made another face, and lowered it.

“You’re popular this morning,” Clara said without looking in his direction.

“Just spam,” he said, tapping the email.

“Are you sure?”

Something in her voice piqued his curiosity and he looked at her. She was fiendishly observing him over her cup of coffee, her eyes expectant and ribbed with that devilish aura he had come to expect when she was scheming something. He looked back at the email and opened it. It was to some sort of website, and looked pretty amateurish; a picture of a forest at night, a clearing, several animals converging in a circle.

“Is this your doing?” he asked bluntly.

Aaron watched the siblings face off with a mixture of amusement and curiosity. If he knew anything, he kept it under his hat. That was Aaron’s way these days, to watch and never to intervene.

“Maybe,” Clara inclined her head, and smiled, breaking her composure. “Alright, yes. I was thinking about last night, our discussion. I know I may have overstepped my limits a bit, but… there’s this website I’ve heard about, it’s for… us.”

“For *us*?” he said, and his hand tightened on the iPhone.

“For shifters. All shifters. You know, it’s hard enough for us to fit into human society. That doesn’t mean that we shouldn’t try or that there aren’t humans out there who do know about us, and who do accept us. We’re not living in the medieval ages anymore.” She gave a look at Aaron, but he was disinterested, and simply sipped at his dark volcanic coffee again. “In any case, it’s designed to let shifters and humans… y’know…”

“Christ, Clara,” he said, and rubbed his brow. He was too tired to even be angry, just fatigued. “This is a bloody dating website. What did you do? Make me a profile?”

She nodded, and her black hair bobbed. “I was very generous, if I do say so myself, I think I capitalized on all of your best qualities. You should thank me. If you're getting emails already, that probably means you have at least a few interested… parties."

Nathan set his phone down and glowered at her. "No."

"Just like that?"

"Just like that," he said. He wanted to feel angrier at her, but he knew that even at her worst, Clara was only ever looking out for him, maybe too much, sometimes. But how could he fault her for that?

She touched her chin and wrinkled her lips. "There is a strategic reason behind me doing this, y'know. It wasn't just a whim or a practical joke," she said. "It will really help your chances with the Pack, give them even more reason to trust you and consider you for the Alpha position… if you look like you're at least interested in getting a mate."

"Dean doesn't have a mate," he pointed out.

"No, that's true. But you can bet his sister is aiming to find him one. This will give you some leverage," she said.

All business then, he thought. "So me going on a date… with a *human*… makes me a better candidate?" he asked, and tried his hardest to put scorn into his voice.

Clara opened her mouth to say something, but it was Aaron who responded first. "Actually, pup, that does make a certain amount of sense."

Both siblings turned at him – since the death of their parents, he had been one of the few Pack members not to voice any real opinions. Nathan had assumed he didn't want to compromise his own position, or else he was simply waiting for the opportune moment to choose sides.

"Clara was right about the Pack moving in new directions. I'm an old wolf, but I'm not that rigid I can't see that change is necessary – imperative, even. We're moving into an age when humans and shifters have to co-exist. Old hatreds die hard they say."

"Meaning what?" Clara said, equally as surprised as Nathan that he was now taking part in a conversation about the leadership.

"Meaning," he winked at Nathan, "that the Pack, and other elders, recognize this fact. You taking the initiative to reach out, to make connections with the human society, well it's a bit of a symbolic gesture. It shows that you are aware of the way in which our own society and race is heading. And it would definitely give you some advantage over Dean."

"I thought you didn't want to get involved in this?" Nathan queried.

Aaron shrugged. "Let's keep it between us then," he said and stood up, turning to leave, "but for the record, Dean wouldn't make half the Alpha you would."

Clara and Nathan watched him go, and each shared a mild look of surprise for the benefit of the other before she finally sat down and braced her chin in one palm. “Damn.”

“I know,” he murmured, and picked up his phone.

The message was simple, curt, and the responder was someone with the tag Nika88. He held up and showed it to Clara, who pursed her lips. He had always had limited contact with humans, even though he’d attended university. Somehow he had always kept himself at a distance from them, as if he was at least subconsciously aware that he could never belong to their world. And here Clara and Aaron both were actively encouraging him to try again.

What’s the worst that could happen? he wondered.

“Alright,” he murmured distastefully, “I’ll try, but no guarantees. Hell, I’m bad enough at trying to talk to girls.”

Clara brightened. “That’s all I ask.”

*

Nathan messaged her and they both agreed to meet at Rouge. In truth, he had very little idea of what to expect. Her profile told him that she was the director of an art gallery, and there was a certain maturity and sophistication, so he chose the fanciest restaurant he knew. Outside the restaurant, he fiddled with his suit and checked his tie in the reflection of the window.

"Are you... Nathan?" a female voice suddenly asked from behind.

He turned abruptly, and saw himself looking at a bright eyed woman. She had on a blue form-fitting dress, and her dark hair was loose as it fell against her back. She had on a navy green canvas jacket over her top and tugged on one elbow shyly. Skinny legs descended from below the knee length hem, wrapped in black stockings, and on her feet – standing out like a sore thumb – were a pair of red Converse sneakers. The style was at once glaring as it was ingenuous.

Her small round face reminded him of an elfin caricature, and her chin, where it dipped low into a tear-dropped shape, held her countenance with a stiffness, something that made her look even more regal in the shadows of the street lights and reflecting luminescence of the restaurant.

She's beautiful, he thought to himself, and was temporarily distracted.

"Er, yes," he said, extending his hand. "I'm sorry. Nika, right? I hope you were able to find this place okay. It's kind of out of the way. But... it has good food."

"No, it's okay," she looked up. "You have... good taste in restaurants."

"You think so?" he rubbed his head. "I honestly didn't know what to choose. I hope this is okay? I have a reservation for us."

She merely nodded, and there was a reticence to her movements that Nathan recognized as suspicion. He recalled that the website they had both used was designed for humans and shifters. *I have no idea what to say,* he lamented.

Inside, the maître'd led them to a table that faced out on the street, and they both awkwardly looked at each other.

"You work at an… art gallery?" he tried.

Nika nodded. "More or less, it's interesting work." She lifted her wine glass to her lips and drank heartily, and Nathan had to smile as he filled it.

Wine is definitely a good choice, he thought absently.

"You like art?"

"A bit. Although I'm not much of an artist."

"What do you do?" she inquired.

He fumbled for a moment, trying to figure out a suitable answer. "Well, right now," he cleared his throat, "I guess you could say I'm in… politics. Hah. My family is a stakeholder in a number of companies so I'm kind of trying to smooth out the wrinkles in the businesses. I'm a complete amateur, I'm afraid." He gave a hesitant laugh.

"Oh!" her eyes raised. "That's impressive."

"Not really. Like your job. It sounds really

interesting, actually. Must be nice, to be surrounded by art all the time… and artists."

She laughed, easing into the conversation. "I guess. Now that you mention it, it isn't too bad, but it doesn't leave a lot of time for socializing." She gestured around the restaurant with her head as if to indicate that going on a date was something that was a bit out of the norm for her.

He grinned and nodded. "Well, I guess we at least have that in common. When I'm not under my sister's thumb – she's trying to groom me to be the head of the family – I usually just bike into the mountains. Solitude is a good salve for too much work."

"That's… that's very true," Nika replied.

"You sound surprised," he observed nervously.

Nika put her glass back down, and flipped a lock of hair over one ear. "To be honest with you, Nathan, the last few dates I've gone on… well, they haven't been great. Most guys are too busy flexing their muscles or their careers to ask honest questions. Or to give honest answers."

He blushed and reached for his wine again. Across the table, she was looking at him, and he thought her expression was rather unnerving at first – like she was trying to deduce a new species she had never seen before. A mixture of curiosity and bewilderment, and he tensed up.

I feel like I'm under a microscope, he thought, and met her gaze. No, that wasn't quite it.

It was more as if she had become so accustomed to a certain set of guys, a certain set of interactions, that she was surprised to find something that didn't fit the mold. *Me*, he mused. At the same time, Nika was not what he had expected at all. Ever since Clara had admitted to creating a profile for him on the dating site, he had met the whole scenario as something impersonal. As Aaron had put it, a way to prove to the rest of the Pack that he was able to integrate human and shifter cultures.

That's the wrong way to go about this, he thought shamefully. This woman was obviously intelligent, and whatever *his* motives had been for accepting this rendezvous, hers were clearly different; more honest, as she would have said.

By the time they finished their food and he had adamantly forced the issue and paid for their bill, they were both laughing. Not the forced laughter of strangers, but something deeper. They had both surprised themselves, and each other. As they walked back outside, she looked up and pointed at the stars that had started to bleed into the atmosphere.

"Well," he said at last, "I suppose I should offer to take you home."

She tilted her head. "You think we've actually progressed that far in our relationship?" she joked. "Besides, I thought you said you had a bike? I don't know how I feel about that…"

He sighed. "If it's any consolation, I only like bikes because they're practical. It's got nothing to do with ego, or looking cool," he returned the joke. "Although, if your roommate sees you pull up on the back of a Ducati, it will *definitely* add to your coolness factor."

She giggled. "Alright, screw it. Why not?"

Nathan reached down and touched her hand, and again they were both surprised by the contact, and each blossomed another blush, to the point they both started laughing again. Not at the fact that they were blushing, but at the fact they had both noticed the other one doing it first.

"We're ridiculous, I think," she said.

"Kind of refreshing," he replied, handing her a spare helmet.

She hopped onto the back of his bike, locking her feet onto the stirrups. Her blue dress hiked up her thighs and she felt the warm summer air brush over them. Absently, she tried to pull the hem of it down, but it was a fruitless venture. If Nathan noticed, he acted the gentleman and didn't say anything or let his eyes wander.

"Ready?" he asked. She nodded, and tucked her hands around his waist.

This feels surreal, he wondered as he pulled out gently into the street and made a left. Behind him he could feel Nika tighten her small arms around him, and lean into his back. He had never had a real girlfriend, not in the sense that most people would have defined it. As the two of them drifted lazily in and out of the night time traffic, Nika giving short directions whether to turn left and right into his ear, he found his thoughts drifting. *Is this what it feels like to have a mate?*

He was almost sad when she tapped his shoulder as they neared a small park, dimly lit and casting silhouettes between the branches of trees. "This is your place?" he asked, stopping by the curb and kicking out the bike's stand.

She handed the helmet back and combed her fingers through her hair. "Nope, but because I had such a good night, I think I'm going to go for a walk… this is one of my favorite places actually."

"You sure you don't want an escort?" Nathan offered.

Again she shook her head. "No, it's okay. I like to be alone sometimes. From what you've told me, you can understand that," she said, and he nodded.

It had been one of the more interesting topics between them, how both of them felt somehow strangled, claustrophobic by too much social interaction. It had been one of the things they both recognized as being responsible for the tenuous connection that had formed between them.

“In that case, I’ll bid you goodnight,” he said.

She nodded and gave a little bow with hands in front of her. Her canvas jacket was unzipped down the front, and her breasts swayed as she stood back up and he started the engine again.

“Oh,” she said after him, “and don’t forget to come and visit me at the gallery!”

He gave a thumb’s up and gently rolled off down the street. In the rearview mirror he watched her gaze after him before heading into the walkway of the park. Part of him wondered how he could possibly retell his night to Clara. She would definitely want to know about it. *No,* he decided, *I think this night will be just mine*. His affinity for Nika had been sudden, and it both alarmed and enlivened him to the possibilities.

There was no way to tell if she was into him on a romantic level. But he wasn’t even thinking that far ahead. Even the notion of having her as a friend was somehow appealing. He didn’t have to conceal his identity from her, and even though his shifter descent hadn’t come up during their conversations, the unspoken recognition of it between them had lent itself to an openness he had only ever really experienced with his sister.

He laughed out loud into his helmet, and heard his voice muffle against the inside of his helmet as he made a slow left turn, following the perimeter of the park. A dash of movement caught his eye in the mirror, and he hit the brakes. Two figures, hooded, entered the park a hundred meters behind him. Nothing threatening about them, but Nathan nevertheless turned off to the curb and looked behind them just as they vanished down one of the paths. He hesitated. Something in their gait, their posture, gave him an eerie feeling. It was amazing how much you could tell from a person by the way they walked, whether they loped slowly with large steps, or shuffled with rigid postures.

They're after something, a voice in his brain warned.

He took off his helmet and switched off the ignition to his bike and walked briskly to the pathway where he'd seen the two strangers disappear. There was nothing. Almost as if they had vanished into thin air and he had imagined the whole thing. It made him even more wary. Most humans lacked the finesse of hunters, and gave themselves away easily. The slap of shoes on pavement, the wasted effort of dragging their soles, the small clumsy nuances he had learned to pick up on.

But there was nothing at all, no sound here. *Maybe I'm just being paranoid*, he thought and hesitated again before walking down the path, both hands in his pockets. He chose a target to walk towards every hundred meters, knowing that if anyone *did* see him he would have the look of someone just out for an evening stroll.

Around him, the trees had a haunting appearance, looming in over the path. A prairie wind kicked up from the east trembled through the leaves, rustling them, provoking a flurry of whispers that descended on him from above. He sniffed, testing for anything out of the ordinary.

Human scents, yes. And something more.

He picked up his pace, and stepped off the stone path, his footsteps cushioned by the grass along the side as he rounded toward one of the smaller paths. A crack of a branch startled him and he froze absolutely still. His keen shifter eyes scanned the dark, but he could pick out no movement. The sound had come from around the next bend. Cautiously, he took his hands out of his pockets and cantered toward the bushes.

Through a veil of twigs and leaves he was able to look into an open clearing, where several paths converged and branched out. First, he saw the two figures. Both of them had their hoods up, a selfsame black, and their hands in their pockets as they marched forward. He could read their intentions at a glance. *Definitely hunting.*

Then he saw whom they were stalking: the back of the canvas jacket, the blue trailing skirt underneath, the idiosyncratic Converse sneakers. Nika was moving slowly, seemingly oblivious, and he could hear her humming something, just audibly enough to drown out the approach of the other figures.

Nathan emerged from the bushes, paralleling their route and keeping himself out of view just as they approached Nika. He saw one of them reach out and grab her shoulder, and she turned wildly, her eyes jutting with fear. The second man said something under his breath, but Nathan didn't catch it as he broke into a spring toward them. In an instant, he saw a white flash as the first assailant pulled a knife from his jacket, and then the sound of the second turning at his approach.

"Help!" Nika managed to scream, and tried to pull away.

The first man, undeterred by Nathan's approach, brought his weapon down toward her. Nathan felt his heart drop into his stomach, expecting the worst but with viper-like reflexes Nika wrenched forward, blocking the arm with the knife, and kicking outwards. Her attacker was surprised and let out a grunt as the sneaker took him in the abdomen.

The second man had turned all of his attention on Nathan though, and as the young shifter leapt forward, bringing up his knees, managed to turn on his heel. Nathan growled low in his throat and brought up his hand against the man's sternum. Something cracked under his fingers, and he got a look at the face behind the hood.

He must have been in his forties, but his face had been rearranged so many times it barely looked human. His nose was like a wad of clay, and both eyes were shadowed by a prominent brow. He swore and brought his own meaty fist down on the side of Nathan's head. Stars brightened behind his eyes as he hit the ground. *Stay awake*, he thought. He shook his head just in time to roll out of the way of the man's foot stomping down on the pavement beside his head, and twirled on his back, kicking upwards. The blow glanced off the man's patella, and he screamed, clutching the injured joint. Nathan was up in a flash and slammed his knee into the brute's face.

Blood gushed onto the pavement, and there was another fracturing sound, like ice on a river cracking with the spring. A sigh, and two-hundred fifty pounds collapsed onto the ground. Nathan swiveled, ready to the meet the second attacker who had regained himself and lunged forward. Nika, trying to escape, had tripped hard and scraped her knee. She turned on her back, and tried to scream again but there was no air left in her lungs.

The knife raised as the first hoodie kneeled above her.

"Help," she managed to voice weakly.

She blinked, and saw another shape lunge against the attacker, and both of them scrambled in the grass. The knife scattered across the pavement, its metallic note ringing out against the night air as she lifted herself up weakly, her wounded leg splayed.

Nathan finally broke away and rolled to one side, crouching low like an animal as he put himself between her and the other man. His hood was thrown back now, and he looked just as feral. He was younger than his unconscious companion, but the same vile and cold-blooded look gleamed in his eyes. His hair was almost as raven as Nathan's, and though his face was young it was plastered with scars, some old and some that looked unnervingly new. He snarled.

"N-Nathan?" Nika blurted, her instincts forcing her to limp toward the knife. She held it with both hands tightly, but the frenetic terror in her face made it impossible for her to diagnose enemy from friend. "Wha…"

"Just stay back, Nika," he warned, his attention fixed on the other man. His muscles tingled under his shirt, and he gave in to the killer instinct of his shifter form, letting it clarify the world around him. Scents seemed to intensify, even his vision became clearer. He spat, tasting blood in his mouth where the other man had clubbed him. "Who are you?" he hissed, "You're a shifter. I can smell it… you may have tried to cover it, but you reek. Who sent you?"

The other man merely ducked his head and his fingers dug into the grass.

"Shifter…" Nika mumbled, confused, "Nathan, who… what is going on??"

He ignored her for the present, watching as this new enemy hunched over, curling as if in pain. Nathan already knew what it meant, but it was still a shock to see a shifter try to transform so conspicuously in a human environment.

The black hoodie seemed to stretch, bubbling outward as the man let out a low whine of pain like a dog. Fur began to grow on the visible parts of his skin, his hands, his cheeks. Bone began to rearrange under the flesh, the sickening clack of cartilage growing and expanding, and flesh stretching against its own elasticity. Finally, there was a rip as the clothes tore at their seams, and more dark fur emerged, dark spikes of it flaring outward.

Nika fell down again, squatting on the grass. All she could do was watch in mute fascination as the shifter bucked forward on the grass and became something else entirely. In moments, it was over, and the new creature struggled up on all four legs, its long muzzle as wide as a cannon barrel, and just as dangerous. Glowing yellow eyes, halfway lupine and halfway human, seethed with hate and the black lips that curled over its long row of teeth glistened with a poisonous intensity.

"If you want to play games," Nathan muttered, pulling his own biker's jacket off and casting it on the ground beside him, "then I'll play. But I don't have any rules."

The dire wolf that had emerged from its human shell pawed the grass, raking its huge claws into the earth in a sort of mutual challenge. Nathan snarled and stooped, placing both his hands on the grass as he prepared to enter his own transformation.

But there was no time. A loud blaring sound echoed through the park, drifting like smoke between the tall trunks and holding itself there. It was long, mournful, like a war horn, and the other shifter suddenly blanched and lifted its head. It snarled, opening its jaws and gnashing them together, and crouched again to leap. A second blast on the horn, and this time the shifter reacted in frustration, shaking the huge slope of its head. It gave a final look at both its quarries and turned brusquely, sprinting off into the darkness of the undergrowth. For several long moments, Nathan didn't move. He sniffed the air again. The scent, thought strong, was lifting.

He stood up and exhaled. Behind him, Nika still held the scavenged blade with both hands, her legs splayed out in front of her. She was shaking visibly, and he swallowed. Suddenly, all of the awkwardness of their first encounter reestablished itself, and they both stared at each other.

"Wh-what was that…" she finally managed.

He stooped, locking his eyes on hers. They both held each other in that private orbit, tethering one another to the moment. If they looked away now, they'd both be lost, irretrievable, and somehow she sensed that.

"That was a shifter," he explained, as calmly as he could, trying to make it sound as matter of fact as possible. The only way to soothe her now would be to normalize what had just happened. *As if that were possible*, he thought. His own brain was already trying to piece the puzzle together. Who had these men been? It was nearly unheard of these days for shifters to attack humans. And wolves, no less. "These were shifters," he said again, "both of them were wolves."

"Wolves," she repeated, "but… but they're… I saw him… change."

He cocked his head. It was one thing to be traumatized by being attacked by strange men but there was incomprehensibility in her voice, as if she'd just encountered something out of fairy tales. In truth, she had.

But surely she knows about our kind – we used the same website after all.

"That's what shifters do," he said, "but I don't know why they were after you. It's okay now; they're gone. It's okay, aright?"

Her face still didn't register anything. "Sh-shifters? What are you talking about??"

"People," he said, and gulped, "like me."

There was a scurrying sound behind, and the older man picked himself up in a daze and sneered at the two of them. Nathan prepared to fight him again, but a third and final horn blow signaled from nowhere, and he hobbled off. Reluctantly, the young shifter watched him go, and turned back to Nika.

She shook her head again and dropped the knife, and his eyes widened as he caught the scent of blood. Nika caught the direction of his gaze and looked down at her stomach. Under the canvas jacket on her left side was a dark wet spot, and a small pale slit of flesh, drenched in bright red. She touched it, staring at the blood on her fingertips without being able to understand. Her eyes blinked rapidly and her mouth opened slightly as she began to loll, and Nathan reached out quickly to catch her as she slumped forward unconscious. He swore and ripped at his sleeve, tearing off a swathe of black fabric.

So much for that suit, he thought without humor, and cradled her head as he leaned her back on the grass.

Gently, he probed the wound. More blood stained his fingers, and he pushed the torn folded sleeve under the slit in her blue dress. The tensile strength of it worked well to keep the makeshift bandage in place, but it was a poor substitute for a surgeon; it was wide, but it didn't look deep. The other shifter must have managed to get in a lucky strike while Nika had been trying to escape. She hadn't even noticed it amid her terror and the cocktail of adrenaline.

Still holding onto her, he reached for his phone, and his fingers left bloody prints on the screen as he speed-dialed Clara. Her raspy voice came through like a godsend.

"Need help, now. Swanson Park, bring the Cadillac," he blurted, "and make sure Aaron is up and sober. He's going to be needed."

CHAPTER THREE

She couldn't remember the dream in its totality. All she knew was that she was running on all fours. Occasionally, she would look down and see her feet – only they weren't feet, they were paws. Grey and furred, and clawed. And she could hear her own breath, a steady rhythm that echoed in her ears as if off the walls of a deep and familiar cavern. The smell of trees; the feel of the sun on her skin.

When Nika awoke, a shelf of light was listing up her legs. Her head hurt terribly, and she her throat felt dry. She turned towards the window, and saw green leaves through an ornate window, double paned and Venetian. A warm smell of lavender came off the white sheets. She closed her eyes again, and tried to recall what had happened. Even memory was like a dream, something that was hard to access, and which had little consequence to reality. *Even though it definitely happened.*

The park; the men in hoodies; the wolf. Her stomach felt cold with the recollection, and she pulled the sheets away. A rectangular bandage was taped over her right side, and when she touched it, she hissed and quickly pulled her hand away. *Blood.* That had been part of it to. She felt panic and stood up, throwing her legs over the side. She had on a new white tank-top, and white pajama shorts, though none of them were hers.

"Where the hell," she managed.

Nathan had been there. Yes, he'd saved her. She remembered that much. But then it was all blank. Her leg was stiff, and she saw another bandage had been placed over her knee. Limping she made her way to the door. The house was extravagant, and paintings and oil portraits lined the walls. After being so accustomed hers and James' cozy bachelor apartment, this place was a veritable mansion.

Curiosity led her down one of the parabolic staircases to the main floor, and she heard voices. Clutching her side she made it to an entryway and braced herself against the frame.

"I know what you wanted to do, Nathan, but do you really think this is a good idea? There's still too much we don't know," a woman's voice admonished.

"They were shifters, Clara," Nathan's young stolid voice interrupted. "That means it's our business. Besides, you really think she'd be safe in a hospital? It wasn't a bad wound, Aaron said it was only the flesh, didn't even make it through the third layer of skin."

"That's not the point—"

"No, Clara, listen. You were the one who signed me up for that website, and I met Nika as a result of it. Now, until I know for certain who those men were, and why they were after her, it's safer to keep her here."

"Even though, according to you, they were *wolves*."

"Not from our Pack," he asserted. "I didn't recognize them… nor their scent. But they were hardened. If I'd had to fight both at the same time, I'd be the one Aaron needed to patch up."

There was a shuffling of footsteps and an exasperated sigh. "This couldn't have happened at a worse time, Nathan. Hell, this has well backfired. I'll try to talk with the elders, see if they have any idea who these unknown assailants are. And why they were after a human."

"It can't have been a coincidence… two shifters try to kill her minutes after I drop her off from a date? No, there's something wrong, Clara. Who else knew I was going out tonight?"

A pause. Nika bit her lip, and put her hand on the doorframe. Her foot slipped on the linoleum and she reached out and clutched at it, letting out a little cry of surprise. Her right side blazed with pain and she doubled over, trying to catch her breath.

Nathan and another woman turned into the hallway and looked down at her in surprise. But it was Nathan who reacted first, reaching under her and propping her up. A faint red splotch appeared on the bandage and she winced.

"Easy now," he whispered, helping her up again, and she put her arm around his neck, "you'll pull your stitches. It's not bad, but you need to rest."

His black sweater rubbed against her arm, and

suddenly his face was very close to hers. She felt small, vulnerable in a way she hadn't felt in a very long time. For so long she had relied only on herself, to the point that to have to depend on another now gave her a sensation of anxiety.

"Nathan," she said, her voice quivering. The beautiful black haired woman across from them crossed her arms. There was a faint resemblance between the two, but marked by very different personalities. *His sister*, Nika thought.

"Here," Nathan replied and helped her into the kitchen and onto a warm sofa couch near a small alcove where a semicircular window opened out onto a garden, with the downtown core of Calgary in the distance. "Drink something, you're probably thirsty," he said, offering her a glass of water.

"Where…"

"Our house," the woman replied sternly, "My name is Clara. Nathan brought you here after you got hurt. We had our in-house surgeon treat you. Nothing serious, but Nathan's right: for now, take it easy."

"Then it's true," Nika said, sating her thirst, "about… about shifters?"

"You didn't know?" Nathan asked. "That website you used to contact me. It's… it's for humans and shifters alike. Our existence is still a secret among the majority of humans… but it's changing. Slowly. I thought you knew."

She shook her head and suddenly remembered she was only in a small tank top and shorts. Her cheeks blushed, and she tried in vain to cover her naked thighs. Clara seemed to anticipate her modesty, and offered her a small quilted blanket, which she wrapped around herself.

"My… my roommate," she said, "son of a bitch. He gave me the website. Probably thought I'd meet someone interesting. He's always trying to make my life more 'interesting'. Kind of neglected to tell me about… my god…"

"Yeah," Nathan and Clara shared a look.

"I'm sorry," she said. "I… it's just… a lot to take in."

"I have to meet Aaron," Clara said, and stood up. Her leather jacket flexed wetly, and she gave another look at the human in her presence. There was nothing inherently malignant about her, but her attitude was still frosty. *Understandably so,* Nika thought, *I've barged into affairs I have no understanding of.* "Keep her out of sight from the others, though I doubt it will be easy to keep her a secret now."

Nathan nodded, his muscular jaw arched. His obeisance to her was evident and staunch. "Just figure out who was after her," he commented as she left, and turned back to Nika.

"I overheard," she said.

"I don't suppose *you* have any idea of why those men

were after you?" he asked, not expecting an answer. She shook her head. "In that case," his face tightened, "I have to take full responsibility for what happened to you. Shifters don't attack humans, not if they can help it. It complicates matters, and is dealt with *very* seriously. Those men were asking for a death sentence from the aligned Packs. I'm… I'm sorry, Nika. This is my fault."

She shook her head again, but she couldn't disagree with him. A few minutes ago she hadn't even known such creatures existed. "Are you… I mean, is this your… natural form?"

He refilled her cup with tea and sat down on a chair opposite her. "Natural is a funny word," he said. "I think both my shapes are natural. It just depends on the circumstance. That doesn't really answer your question does it?"

She managed a smile. "No, that was a good answer," she paused, "so… you look like… like that other one?" Fear crept into her voice, and she turned her head away, embarrassed, but Nathan only smiled that boyish grin again.

"I'd like to think I'm more handsome," he joked. "Our wolf shapes are determined by our human shapes, and vice versa. Admittedly, I'm not quite as nightmarish or intimidating as our mutual acquaintance in the park."

"And… and this place is yours?"

He looked around, shrugging at the décor. "Well, my parents. But Clara and I grew up here."

"Clara…"

"My sister," he said, and saw her relax. "She looks mean, and she can be. But she's just worried about you, that's all. There's a lot of family politics going on right now, things that could be put in jeopardy by what happened last night."

"Your family business," she groaned, "what exactly?"

"Nothing shady," he teased. "We're not the Cosa Nostra or anything. Legitimate businesses, mostly tech and IT stuff. But the politics I'm talking about have more to do with leadership. We're wolves, although there are many kinds of shifters. But right now our Pack is in the middle of an… I guess you might call it an election."

The inscrutable hesitation in his voice caught her attention. "Wolves elect their leaders?"

He shrugged. "Didn't use to. But yes, we're very *modern* now," he said, but the bottom had fallen out of his voice. "The truth is, my parents used to be the Alphas. Mostly a titular title, that doesn't really have anything to do with the way the family and the business runs these days. But that doesn't mean the role of Alpha isn't a powerful one. It's rooted in tradition."

"Then… then your parents…" He looked to one side,

and she felt as if she'd put her foot in her mouth. "Never mind, I'm sorry… that's rude. I'm just trying to make sense. I think my brain is still frazzled," she apologized.

"It's okay," he assured her, "They died. And that's where I come in. I'm one of the candidates."

Nika puffed her cheeks out. Part of her was aware of the fact she was taking this calmly. Another part knew the only reason she wasn't freaking out was because it was all so much of an overload that her body didn't know how to react except to accept the reality of her situation at face value. She wrapped the blanket around herself tighter and leaned back against the couch.

"Are you okay?" he asked.

"I'll level with you, Nathan," she said, "you're the best and worst date I've ever had."

He wrinkled his brow, not quite sure how to take it, as a compliment or as an insult, but he suspected there was legitimate cause for both depending on perspective. "I *will* figure this out," he said, "I can promise you that much. In the meantime, though—"

"I heard," she held up her hand, "safer here. I can't hardly argue, can I?"

"Well, you could," he looked timidly toward the doorway where Clara had disappeared, "but do you *really* want to argue with my sister?"

She closed her eyes. *Fuck.* "In that case, I think I need another cup of tea."

He reached for the teapot and she extended her hand, her fingers catching on his sleeve. She gulped again, grappling with that sense of vulnerability she had trained herself so hard to escape from but it was different with Nathan. For Nika, dependency on someone was rooted in fear. Fear that person would let her down, that she would invest too much in them and be betrayed, that she would somehow lose whatever strength she had accumulated by allowing herself to rely on another.

Why am I so comfortable then? she wondered, and when he turned to look at her, she closed her mouth.

He touched her hand and wrapped his own around hers. His touch was warm and dry, coarse with the calluses of workingmen – or of wolves running on all fours, she thought – and yet unmistakably tender. *As if afraid of its own strength,* she blushed again, felt her heart beat trammel against the walls of her chest, and lowered her eyes.

"When I say *tea,*" she murmured at the ceramic pot, "I mean something a *lot* stronger than that."

Nathan opened his mouth in an *ah* shape. "I think that can be arranged. Although, if Clara finds out I've been medicating my patient on rum, we'll *both* be patients."

CHAPTER FOUR

It was relatively easy to convince her manager to take several weeks' vacation time. The fact that Nika hadn't taken a single sick day since she'd starting working at the gallery had given her plenty of leeway, and she frowned as she clicked her phone shut. *They almost sounded happy to give me time off*, she reflected, and it was another realization of how much work had consumed her life. She still felt anxious, cooped up in Nathan's mansion, but somehow it felt nice to take it easy for once. Nathan had given her a whole room in the west branch to herself, and she almost felt as if she were at some resort.

It had been a little more difficult to assuage James' fears. In the end, she had had to admit that she was more or less *involved* with Nathan – she felt silly saying it out loud, but the fib worked well enough and James finally conceded. When she hung up the call, though, she clutched her phone to her chest and bit her lip. Yes, she'd lied. But at the same time, she wondered if there wasn't some sliver of truth in what she'd said. The word *involved* could mean a lot of things.

She touched her stomach, where the wound was healing nicely. The morning sun was coming down between two tall Douglas fir trees, scattering the light in a diffraction that echoed through the garden. The smell of lupines lifted to the air, and she breathed it in. Her second day at Nathan's, she'd met Aaron, a kindly old man with a permanent five o'clock shadow of grey bristly hair on his chin and cheeks, and eyes that were almost glacial. Nika had been told he was the one who had stitched her up, and it immediately inclined her toward the old man. Even though he was accommodating, and other than Nathan, the only one who didn't seem to mind her invasion into the privacy of the mansion, she would still sometimes have to stop and remind herself that he, too, was a wolf.

He was busy at the moment down the path, stooped over a bed of roses as he trimmed them with elegant snips. Nika finished sipping her coffee and set it down on the white enameled paint of the cast-iron table and stood up shakily. She smoothed her blue nylon shorts and wrapped her long hair into a bun as she limped toward him. He didn't look up as she approached, but his voice crackled like snow freezing in the night air.

"Shouldn't get up, miss," he said, his face still buried among his roses. "You're a strong one, I grant that. For a human, you got a will to heal, but my work on you probably doesn't appreciate you moving around too much."

Nika touched her side again. It was still stiff, but the pain was minimal. "That's what Nathan keeps saying too, but you know I'm fine. It was only a flesh wound."

"Could've been worse," Aaron growled, and snipped another loose branch.

"I know, but I can't just sit around… I need to *do*

something."

"Best you don't *do* anything. You know what the situation is in the house. And you know how much pressure Nathan is under. The best thing for you, and for him, is for you to get better."

"Trying to get rid of me?" she teased, and kneeled down beside him on the grass.

He sighed. "Actually, I rather enjoy your presence. It seems to keep Nathan centered and focused, most of the time. And you make a good buffer for Clara. That girl is even more wound up than her brother," he took in a breath, "but as for the rest of the Pack, you're definitely a subject of interest."

She knew he was referring to some of the other people she'd seen wandering around the mansion, though she tried her best to keep to the west side and avoid them. Still, she was avidly aware of the glances and whispers she evoked. Nathan had been very reticent to talk about it, but she'd gathered they were other members of the same wolf clan. There was one who was a huge body-builder type named Dean. Another gave her the creeps; a skinny and tenacious woman with big eyes and a nervous sort of temperament that reminded Nika of a stray dog, something opportunistic and cunning, waiting for the right opportunity to strike out.

"Has there been any word about… about who attacked me?" she asked after a pause.

"Not as of yet. But Clara should be returning soon. I know she's been looking into it. It's got all of us worried," he held a finger to his lower lip, "especially considering your relationship to Nathan."

She blushed. "Relationship? We went out on a single date," she said defensively.

There was more to it, she knew. Since having been more or less relegated to the mansion grounds for fear of another attack on her life, she and Nathan had spent almost every day together. She had gotten used to his company. But certainly there was nothing romantic, was there? She touched her breastbone, surprised at the lightness that suddenly lifted up from her stomach.

Aaron shrugged. "Guess I'm old fashioned, haha," he smirked. "You and him do make a good couple though, for what it's worth. But don't worry, Nathan promised to get to the bottom of this – that lad will. You'll be back to your own life before you know it."

She smelled one of the roses. It was a bright red, almost blood-like with the sunlight sifting through its thin petals.

"I *have* enjoyed it here," she said, more to herself, "but I think Nathan still feels… guilty."

"That boy always takes the world on his shoulders," Aaron contemplated, "and since the death of his parents, it's only been him and Clara. He feels the pressure of that. Forced to grow up a lot quicker than he probably wanted to. But don't let it get to you… none of this was your fault or his."

"Try to convince *him* of that," Nika rolled her eyes. Her dark hair caught the sunlight as she leaned back on the grass and a slant of sun coursed through it, ribboning with hints of dark red.

Aaron laughed again.

"Probably futile, you're right," he patted the dirt off his knees. "Okay, if you're that insistent, then I guess I have no choice in the matter. If you want to help an old man with his roses, I'd be much grateful for the help."

Nika beamed and nodded, and followed him towards the adjacent clump, which were by contrast a deep snow white. Aaron was careful to prevent her from straining herself, but by noon, both of them were coated in dirt and chuckling at private jokes they'd managed to mythologize out in the garden. He stooped into the kitchen and waved at her.

"Go on and clean up, I'll fix us some sandwiches," he urged.

In the shower, she scrubbed her body clean, careful to avoid the water-proof bandage on her stomach. Dirty water pooled at her feet and she lifted her head toward the jet of hot water. Against her will, one of Aaron's comments floated to the surface of memory, his comment about her and Nathan being a good couple together. She didn't think of him in that way, she thought. No, it was more like he had become a dear and trusted friend, someone she had learned to trust.

For me, I guess that's a pretty big accomplishment, she let out a small laugh as she combed the water through her hair.

Nathan was cute, she had to admit. And there was that same ripped muscular quality that all his family seemed to have inherited, a hunter's physique. And he was different. She laughed again and felt self-conscious, giggling to herself in the shower. *Fair enough James,* she said, *you've definitely made my life more interesting.*

She was still smiling when she stepped out of the shower and wrapped a towel around herself. As soon as she turned around the corner to her room though she gasped and jumped back, almost dropping her cover, and fumbled quickly to keep it over her breasts.

A thin-faced woman was staring back at her, arms crossed. She had on low-riding jeans, an overly large belt holding it to the jutting bones of her hips. A burnished silver buckle nestled above her navel, which peeked out from a jean-jacket vest and white tank-top. Nika knew her name but only by reputation, one of Nathan's cousins. *Flores.*

"Ah, I'm… I'm sorry," Nika murmured, even though she knew the other woman was at fault. This had been assigned as her bedroom, after all. "C-can I help you?"

Flores piercing gaze didn't falter and she took a step forward, pointed leather boots scuffing the carpet. "Just wanted to get a look at you," the skinny woman replied. Her face was even more hawkish than Clara's, and while the latter had a certain grace and lively beauty, this other woman seemed sharp for sharp's sake. Her short pixie-hair cut took years off her age, only to have them restored by the sunken shape of her eyes and the faint wrinkles creasing inward. "Our little human on the premises. I finally get a good look at you. What's your name, human?"

"Nika," she managed.

"What a lovely name," Flores slipped into a saccharine supplication. "You really should know better, though. Most humans wouldn't dare step foot into a wolf's den. That is what this place is, you know?"

Nika gulped. "I… this is my room," she murmured.

"*Your* room?" Flores smiled two sets of gleaming white teeth. "On the contrary, my dear, you're inhabiting areas that are so far from your own kind you might as well be in the woods. And you know what happens when a human goes into the woods?" Nika shook her head, and Flores smiled again.

"If you don't mind, I'd like to change."

"By all means," Flores opened her arms inviting her

in, but made no move to leave herself.

"Alone, if that's okay," Nika tried to put some strength into her voice, and took a step forward.

The other woman was too quick though, and Nika felt strong hands grip her arm and toss her toward the bed against one wall. It was well aimed, but she still let out a grunt as she hit the mattress, and cupped her hand to her side.

"Little bitch," Flores mouthed, and slapped her hands together.

Nika's face contorted in fear again. Her towel had ripped off and was sprawled on the floor. She put one hand across the glancing angles of her breasts and her other palm tried in vain to cover the dark pubic triangle between her legs.

"Well, well," Flores crossed her arms again.

For a tiny woman, she had remarkable strength. *No, not woman, a wolf*, Nika reminded herself, and grit her teeth. Once again, she felt vulnerable – but it wasn't like before in the park. There she had been afraid, terrified even, but a subconscious part of her mind had been resigned to the fact that at least Nathan was there to protect her. Here, now, she was utterly alone.

"Please, leave me alone," she pleaded.

Flores sneered. "I wanted to get a real look at you.

See what Nathan found so goddamn appealing," she gazed down lecherously at Nika, "I have to admit, definitely something attractive. But you're still only a human. Weak."

Nika's whole body felt as if it were on a bed of ice. She could scarcely move, let alone fight back. Her naked body began to tremble, and she clutched her breasts tighter, curling her legs over one another. "Please," she murmured.

Flores made a low growling sound in her throat and approached the bed, her boots again tracing over the carpet, and there was something nearly fox-like about her movements. Up close, she was even more fearsome. Her small pointed nose was turned up at the end, just enough to give her a childishly snub appearance, except that, matched with her very adult eyes, the composition was unnerving.

She was about to say something more when another voice interrupted, harsh and commandeering, and laced with threat. "What the fuck is going on?" Clara snarled from the doorway.

Her hands were on her hips, that proto-leather Goth outfit again, like some sort of biker chick out of an 80's movie. There was no evident malice in her voice, but as she looked first at Flores and then back down at Nika naked and cowering on the bed, her face froze.

"Nothing, cuz," Flores said sweetly, and put her hands behind her back, trying to act innocent. "Me and the human were just having a chat. Nothing special. I accidentally caught her out of the shower though… it's just us girls though, no problem."

Clara looked to Nika for confirmation, and didn't find it. "This room is off-limits," she said, stating an ultimatum. "The next time I find you here, if I hear you've been within ten yards of this room again, we'll have words, Flores."

Flores tried to act cool and opened her mouth to retort, but her voice quaked. "Of course, Clara. As you said, this human is under your protection. I wouldn't dream of harming her. You have so little faith in me, don't you? Tssk! Now, now," she bent toward Nika again, and an overwhelming smell of some cheap perfume struck her like the spines of a nettle. "I'm not all bad, am I?"

"Leave," Clara said.

That single word rang out like a bell tone, and Flores didn't wait to hear it echo as she slithered past the older shifter, still standing immobile in the doorway. There was an evident struggle of their auras as they met, but it was Flores who seemed to duck her head in a conciliatory act of deference. Or perhaps, fear.

It was only after the click of her heels on the tiles had disappeared that Clara sniffed and entered, slowly shutting the door. Without a word she walked toward the bed and knelt, and handed the fallen towel to Nika.

"Thank you," Nika managed.

"You've been making friends," Clara raised an immaculate eyebrow, "although I could take affront to your choice of friends. What did she say to you?"

Nika uncovered her fair breasts and accepted the towel, pulling it around her midriff and hugged her ankles, trying to hide her own sex from the eminent she-wolf. "She… I don't know what she wanted," she replied.

Clara nodded. "Next time she tries anything, you come to me," she said. "I'll handle her."

The sudden and immediate warmth that grew between them originated out of a self-same wariness or hatred for Flores, and yet Nika appreciated it. It was like having a big sister, even though she knew even less about Clara than she did about Nathan.

"Thank you," she said again. "I… I know this is a burden. On everyone."

Clara looked at her apprehensively. "On *us*? Ah, dear, you were the one attacked by shifters. This is more of an inconvenience to you than to us, believe me. And don't pretend it isn't, I've seen you the last few days… you're very good at putting on a brave face, trying to act like everything is normal. It's a credit to you, but I can see through it."

Since coming to the mansion, Nika had done her best to try and integrate all this new information into her consciousness: the existence of werewolves, the inner workings of a species and culture outside of her own human one. But it had been difficult, and she hated to admit it, least of all to someone else. Clara's probing glance was surgical, as if she'd cut to the very core of Nika's own aggregate of fear.

"How... how did you know?"

A smile formed on Clara's lips as she sat down beside the girl on the bed and looked at both of their reflections in the mirror across the room. "Let's just say that one good kind deserves another. I'm very stubborn about 'fessing' up to it, but you and I are more similar than you think. That's... that's probably why I've been regarding you so coldly," she inclined her head, "and for that I'm sorry."

"It's okay," Nika replied. "I suppose... I'd feel the same way, in your position."

"My position?"

Nika blushed. "Just... I mean, you and Nathan. I can tell he really looks up to you. And you really try to protect him, even from himself. I can only imagine how hard a job that is, heh."

Clara nodded. "I guess we're both transparent," she sighed.

"Or, just reflective of one another," Nika offered. "I hope I'm not this see-through to Nathan and Aaron as I am to you. It has been difficult; I won't lie. And I'm still afraid. I don't even know what to feel most days, it's like there are two of me now: one part is still trying to live in the past, with the simplicity of a job and debt and roommates and all that bullshit, and the other is… I dunno."

Clara stood up went to the window. "You got more than you bargained for, that's for sure," she admitted. "I was actually looking for you before I found Flores in here. And the fact it was Flores makes things even more complicated."

"What do you mean?" Nika asked, and sat up on her knees.

"I'd prefer to tell you and Nathan together, actually… and, somewhere else, where the walls don't have ears, if you get my meaning," Clara gave a subtle wink.

Nika dressed hastily, throwing on another borrowed pair of jeans and a button-up plaid shirt that hugged her abdomen and chest in a perfect parabola. She had often wondered *whose* bedroom she had appropriated since coming here, and it was only when Clara had sat down next to her that Nika had guessed it. The same scent that seemed to linger on the wardrobe of clothes – sweetness like fresh hay, but also the darker tones of earth and feminine sweat – had come off Clara.

She was right, Nika thought, *even though she's been cold to me and tried to keep her distance, she was still the one who gave up her own room for me to use*. Her mind returned to Flores and she felt a sick wringing in her stomach, wondering what might've happened if Clara hadn't barged in.

Downstairs, both sister and brother were waiting for her, and Nathan smiled as he put a finger to his lower lip and reached down to grip her hand, leading the two of them after Clara who was already barging headlong toward one of the side doors that opened out into the garden.

The sun was still shining, but had come up higher above the trees, and she felt the warmth of it blister against her bare skin as they skirted across the open lawn and headed toward one of the smaller adjacent out-buildings. The shack was where Aaron kept all his tools, an age-blackened little thing that was idiosyncratic to the rest of the house. The door creaked open as Clara ushered them in and shut it behind them again, peering through the dust-stained window to make sure they hadn't been followed.

The smell of old motor oil, of rust, and sawdust was a stark contrast to the lavender and overly hygienic décor of the rest of the mansion. Nika was surprised to see Aaron already inside, squatting on one of several plastic empty milk crates, and a makeshift table of car-tires and plywood holding a plate of sandwiches and iced tea. Nathan urged Nika to sit down and let go of her hand while Clara stood at the door with her arms crossed.

"Have a sandwich," Aaron suggested, trying to lighten the mood.

“What’s this about?” she asked, accepting one of them, and surprised at her own hunger.

Nathan rubbed his pant leg. “That’s your cue, Clara,” he said. “What did you want to tell us that requires us hiding out in the toolshed.”

She stopped look out the window and uncrossed her arms. “I’ve been spending the last few days corroborating things with other Packs across the country, and even a couple of the nomadic groups down in the States, trying to piece all of this together,” she said, and took a breath trying to organize her thoughts. “I think we were all underestimating just how important this new leadership race will be, not just to our Pack, but to the rest of our kind as well. Our parents… I think they tried to be modest, but the fact is we’ve got a lot of sway, our family. More than we’ve been led to believe.” She gazed across the table at Aaron who licked his fingers and made an innocent face. “You knew, didn’t you, Aaron?”

A muscle in Nathan’s jaw tightened. “What are you onto, Clara? What’s Aaron got to do with this?” he said tensely.

Aaron held up a weathered hand. “It wasn’t my place to say,” he directed his voice at Clara, “and still isn’t. But I guess there’s no point in trying to hide it now. Nathan, there’s a lot your parents didn’t tell you about us, about the Pack. Things that they wanted to keep a secret, lest they fall into the hands of the wrong people.”

“Wrong people,” it was Nika who whispered.

“Wrong people being those two brats the two of you know so well,” he pointed his finger at Nathan and Clara, “but there are others, other members of the Pack. Other groups, even other shifters.”

“What are you talking about?!” Nathan interrupted.

Aaron looked at his sandwiches, selected another one from the plate, and bit into it, the cucumber crunching under his teeth. He gestured at Nika instead, and his eyes were keen and strangely wise. “Tell me, Nika, as an outsider, someone who has no precedent for shifter culture, for someone who has only recently discovered such creatures as us even exist, what do you know of shifters? Of werewolves?”

Nika gulped, and Nathan’s bundled fists relaxed. “Only the normal stories, y’know.”

“Tell us.”

“That normally you’re all human, but during the full moon you turn into wolves. Sometimes you can turn into wolves without the full moon,” she said, feeling useless.

“And, what happens if we bite you?”

At this, Nathan turned furiously toward the old man, but kept his mouth shut. Nika swallowed again, it felt as if her throat were swollen, something hard pressing against it. She touched her neck and tried to finish talking. "Legends say, I guess, that you become one. A werewolf, I mean."

Clara held up her hand. "Enough of this pattering around the issue. Just tell them, Aaron."

His hoarse throat sounded like a blunted instrument as he spoke. "Among us shifters, stories have always inflated the truth of things. In fact, we don't change during a full moon. We may feel more strongly driven during those lunar phases, but there's nothing mystical about it," he stopped, "but some things, the stories do get right. It's a secret that's been kept by our family for centuries and for centuries we've never had to worry about it, especially with human and shifters interacting more and more.

"But in the past, things were not… pleasant. Most of our history has been oral, and so much of it has been lost. What there is of it, however, did manage to survive but among humankind; namely, that of a monster who looks like a wolf. And whose bite can turn its victims into that selfsame monster."

"Rubbish," Nathan spat, "that's an old wives tale."

"Have you ever bitten a human?" Aaron offered with a coy wrinkling of his brow. The young shifter ducked his gaze. "The benefit of being only an 'inflated myth' is that very little stock is put in it. There have been hardly any attacks from shifters on humans in the last half century."

"But there *have* been attacks," Nathan pointed out,

"even our parents spoke about it. Up in Alaska, where the rogue packs used to live. I've never heard of anyone becoming a shifter from another shifter biting them."

Aaron nodded. "You wouldn't," he replied, "it was the prerogative of your parents – in fact, of your family lineage – to protect that secret. Unfortunately, before either of you could be inducted into that circle of secrets, your parents died. And I was the only one left… that is, until Clara here started digging into history. I counted on that."

"And if I hadn't stumbled on the fact that you and our parents had been lying to us?" Clara said stiffly, frowning at the uncle who had, in a passive way, betrayed them.

"Never any doubt in my mind that you would," he said, evading the question. "It was something you needed to come upon for yourselves."

"Let me get this straight," Nika said, again feeling like the odd man out; these were shifter matters were hardly the place for humans. And yet, all eyes settled inward on her, waiting patiently, courteously for her to continue, "that part of the legend is true? If a shifter… if a shifter bites you, you turn into one?"

"Not precisely," Aaron said, "the theriomorphic gene allows all shifters to transmute according to their specific lineages: bears become bears, foxes become foxes, cougars become cougars. But with wolves, there is a slight augmentation. Call it a genetic accident, something that evolution came across by accident, and then decided to stick with.

"In wolf shifters – and only in specific Pack lineages – there is a residual genetic tag-on which manifests itself as a kind of venom. Think of it like rabies, except it doesn't affect the host at all. Doesn't affect humans either, unless they're bitten, quite deeply, by one of us. It's actually quite difficult to pass the transgenic disease."

"I have rabies," Nathan stated flatly.

"I said *like* rabies," Aaron pointed out, "open your ears, pup."

"Why all the secrecy though?" Nika said, "And why are we…"

"In a shack," Nathan finished her sentence grimly.

Clara glanced back out the window again, turned back toward them. "Our parents, Nathan, they were meant to protect the secret of this… this compound that we carry, it's recessive."

"Meaning," Aaron continued, "that only some members of the Pack carry it. I know for a fact that both you and Clara, do."

"Are there any others?" Nathan asked.

"No," there was relief in the old wolf's voice, "it was also recessive in me. And it didn't pass onto any of the others in our family, Dean and Flores included.

It's just the two of you."

Clara nodded. "If other Pack members knew, they'd be able to turn it into a weapon. If other shifters period knew, they'd be trying to hunt us down for the same reason. The unique adaptation of this... disease we carry, it could be used to create a whole army of shifters."

The potential consequences took a moment to hit Nathan and he stood up, trying to hide his dismay. Nika wanted to go to him and stood up as well, but a hard look from Clara froze her in her steps. The meaning was clear: *leave him alone for this*. Aaron turned his attention back to another sandwich, and the sound of his eating was unbearably loud as all three of them waited for Nathan to say something, anything.

At last, he stretched out his arms and clamped them down on top of his head.

"And you don't want your children to know about this," he pointedly asked the old wolf sitting on the milk crate, and Aaron swallowed and wiped his chin, "why?"

"You need a reason, pup?" he asked back, "Dean wouldn't know what to do with that information, or wouldn't care, which would suit us all fine... but Flores..." An uneasy stricture hardened between him, Clara, and Nika without any of them saying a word. "Besides, this wasn't my side of the family meant to carry the secret, nor protect it. It was yours. And you're the only two left to represent it."

"That still doesn't answer Nika's question," Nathan said, not fooled by the diversion, "why are we out here?"

"I have reason to believe that the two shifters who attacked Nika," Clara stepped in, "might've been affiliated with our Pack. I don't know how, they certainly weren't part of our group. But they might've been hired. These are just whispers, you understand, but I think someone is trying to make sure you don't become the Alpha."

"To what end?" he persisted.

"It's possible someone else… someone in our family… has also come across our parent's legacy," Clara said, "in which case, they might try to use it against us. Those two shifters that were in the park, Nathan, what if they weren't after Nika at all… what if that was all a prelude, a trap to try and lure you out? What if they were really after you, all along?"

Nathan blanched, and his face turned the same color as Aaron's white roses as he reached out and gripped the woodwork bench beside him.

"It's conceivable that since the two of you carry this gene, other interested parties would try and kidnap one or both of you. Extract whatever samples they could. Who knows, anything is possible." Aaron threw up his hands.

The young shifter crossed his arms, imitating his sister. "Right," he said, "well, at least there's some good news in all of this." He smiled at Nika, who suddenly didn't feel hungry at all. "At least you can go home. If Clara's right, they're not interested in you at all."

Nika opened her mouth in protest, but Clara stopped her. "Or they'll just try to use her again," she countered, "since, by accident or design, we've made it appear as if you care about her a great deal. You saved her in the park, you brought her here, you've been protecting her all along. I find it hard to believe that whoever these assailants are, they aren't aware of these facts. And if Aaron and I are right, and the conspirator is closer than we think – part of the Pack, even – that's almost a dead certainty."

Nathan's jaw tightened again, and Nika knew he was fumbling. He'd been thrown between two walls that were ever so slowly crushing him from either side, and there was no way up and no way down. He brushed a lock of black hair out of his eyes in frustration. "So whatever we choose now, it doesn't matter. Damned if we don't, damned if we do, is that it, Clara?" he almost shouted, and then remembered himself and instantly lowered his voice again.

Clara took one step toward him and rapped her knuckles hard against his head and he flinched in pain. "Dumb little brother," she scolded, and it was done with such tenderness that both Aaron and Nika had to smile to themselves in earnest, "of course we *do* something. But we have to make sure what we do is the right thing. If we're not careful we'll not only blow your chance for leadership, which will make us *both* vulnerable afterwards, if someone tries to pick us off, but we'll also get both you and Nika killed in the process. No, there's another option."

"Which is?" Nika asked, standing up again.

"You've already been through enough," Clara said softly, and put an arm on her shoulder.

"No," Nika shook her hand off, "no, you were right, earlier. About me. I'm still scared, even if I'm good at pretending I'm not. But for the first time in my life that's alright. I've always been good at protecting myself, and I'm not so stupid as to assume I don't need help this time around but I'm inextricably linked to this situation, now, whether you or I like it."

The dark haired woman's sudden flair and stalwartness caused Clara to uncross her arms. She wasn't looking at the diffident and confused human that had ended up, bleeding and unconscious, on the mansion's kitchen floor.

"If I go back to my normal life now," she gave Nathan a compassionate look, "it's not like I can just turn off what's already happened to me. I hate to say it, but you made me grow out of that life, it's too small for me to fit into it again. The only choice I have now is to keep moving forward."

"It's too dangerous," Aaron said, shaking his head.

"Life is dangerous," Nika responded quickly. "You want to know who's after the two of you, then I'm your best chance of finding out." She crossed her arms like the siblings, and they both dropped their arms.

Aaron suddenly broke into laughter and took the last sandwich off the tray. "Guess that settles it," he said, and slapped his knees again like he did when he was gardening. "We're all in for the long game. But we can't stay here, it's too dangerous at the mansion."

"What do you suggest, old wolf?" Nathan asked.

"We can't just send Nathan and Nika away somewhere. That would be like conceding defeat over the Alpha position of the Pack. And that's probably exactly what the snake in our midst is hoping for, especially if it's someone in our family, someone who stands to benefit from Nathan *not* getting the leadership," Clara added, although no one in the room wanted to say Flores' name out loud.

A pained expression still crossed Aaron's face. The others wouldn't implicate his own daughter in a possible conspiracy but it was something that crossed all of their minds. He gave a timid smile, as if recognizing their propriety.

"If it's not safe here," he said, "and we still want to give Nathan a fighting chance with the election, then I suggest we bring this whole affair to a bit more of a public domain."

Clara and Nathan both shook their heads, confused by his enigmatic suggestion. "I don't know what that means," Clara admitted.

"I say we call a public forum – all of the related packs and elders – to meet together. It's not a conventional way of doing things, but it is one of the more ancient practices we have. It can't be denied when called. It will allow us to meet at a place of our choosing, one of the ancestral homes. But it will also increase security, making it much harder for anyone to try and compromise Nika or Nathan."

Nika had to admire Aaron. You wouldn't think it to look at him, but he had all the élan of a politician and the charisma and cunning of a diplomat. Clara looked out the window, and rubbed her finger on the glass. "Guess that settles it," she repeated Aaron's words.

CHAPTER FIVE

That night was, ironically, a full moon. Recognizing the irony of it only made Nika shake her head at how sublimely surreal her life had become. She folded her arms across her chest as she looked out on Calgary, the only place she had ever really known. The moon was almost above the cityline now, huge and ominous like a dilated eye, and she touched the blinds and let the darkness enfold the room but only for a moment. The burnt whiff of a match came to life as she lit several of the candles on the wardrobe, the bedside table, and on the mantle above the bed.
Sprawled out on the bed, she stared at the ceiling. She had called James to let him know she would be absent for a while, and his response when she told him where she was going had been almost hysterical. According to Aaron, the Pack that Clara and Nathan belonged to could trace their ancestry to a shifter clan that had once roamed the Alaska coast – and that's where the new forum was slated to take place.

There was a knock on her door and she sat up straight.

"Yes?" she asked, remembering her encounter with Flores.

"It's me," Nathan's familiar voice beckoned.

She visibly relaxed. "It's okay, come in," she said,

and Nathan slowly opened and stepped inside.

"Sorry, I didn't mean to bother you." He came and sat down beside her, right where Clara had sat hours earlier. *They really are siblings*, Nika thought. "I just wanted to check on you to see how you were doing."

Nika inhaled deeply. "Surviving, heh," she said.

"I feel like I really owe you a better date," Nathan offered. "Maybe after all of this is over, unless, of course, this has put you off dating strange guys who turn out to be werewolves for good. In that case, there's not much I can really do."

She laughed. "No, it's not like that." She reached down and put her own hand on top of his, and his eyes widened when he looked up at her. "You've… I mean, Clara, and Aaron, both actually, they told me how hard you've been trying to help me. And I know you blame yourself for this, since—"

"It *is* my fault," he said sternly.

"No, no, it isn't." She squeezed his fist until it relaxed and her fingers slipped between the cracks of his own. "I really… don't know where I'd be without you, Nathan. Granted, the circumstances are… I don't know the word…"

"Fucked," he said, and broke the gravity of his own countenance.

"Fucked, yes," she said, "but that's okay. Weirdly, I

don't think I've ever connected with someone more. Heh, what do you suppose that says about me?"

"That you can't be summed up in one word," he offered and turned his hand over, tracing his own fingers over hers.

Nika gulped and met his eyes, and her heart leapt again. They had been close like this numerous times in the past few days, but never like this, never in such an intimate setting, and she opened her mouth and found she didn't know what to say. She didn't have to. Suddenly, he leaned forward and before she knew it, his lips planted against hers.

Her first instinct, she knew, would be to back away. But for some reason she remained immobile, paralyzed by the sensation that was both pleasurable and terrifying. He moved closer to her, his hand touching her shoulder and moving down, and it was like having an electric current flow across her limbs. She made a little moan, and opened her mouth, moving her own lips against his, and nearly gasped when she felt his tongue slide between them. It was warm and fickle, and darted in and out of her mouth, and she opened wider, letting him explore the dark wet cavern of her mouth.

Nathan leaned her down gently, and she felt her head hit the pillow as he turned his head and sucked on her tongue.

"Uhn, Nathan," she murmured as he pulled away, his lips moving down her chin and her neck. She tilted her head back, giving in to a latent desire. It was a passion she hadn't even been aware of until this moment, like the shadow of something you couldn't see until it was illuminated from behind.

His hand moved lower, sliding over her breasts and she spread out both arms beside her, gripping the sheets and biting her lower lip. His touch was gentle but firm, and before she knew it, she could feel his fingers moving up under her shirt, stroking her stomach, the small minute white hairs on her skin rising with the static.

"Is this okay?" he asked, drawing back for a moment, his voice a whisper.

She opened her eyes and gave a little nod, pulling her shirt up higher. His fingers traced the bottom edge of her blue bra, and she shivered, her stomach muscles flinching.

Nathan undid the buttons on his own shirt, and slid one arm out and then the other. She had seen him, occasionally, without a shirt on while the two of them had been living under the same roof. But never like this. His abdomen ribbed with muscles, lean and taut, and against her own volition she reached out to stroke them, her fingers rising and falling with each jutting ridge of flesh. He smiled, offering himself to her, and she rubbed her hand against his pectoral muscle. Everything about him was solid, granite-like, and yet warm.

His own hands rubbed her ribs and stomach again as

he perched on one arm and explored her by touch. She only let out a little whimper as his fingers teased below her bra again, and then move underneath. She sighed, leaning into him, and he began to massage her breasts, causing her to stiffen. Her nipple hardened immediately, and he let the pink nub of it slide between two of his fingers as he excited her further.

"You're so soft," he murmured.

"And you're so hard," she snapped back with a grin, her nails running up his abdomen.

"Can I go lower?" he asked, moving his fingers to her navel, and then the lip of her jeans.

She stared at the button of her pants and just nodded, and her hands tightened again on the sheets, wrenching them. Nathan smiled and fumbled gingerly with the top button until it slid loose, and then slowly pulled the zipper down. Her panties were the same color as her bra, a robin's egg blue, and he pushed his fingers over top of the fabric. She gasped again and clutched at her breasts with one hand, and Nathan's fingers trailed over her pubis. She was already wet, and a dark spot had formed between her legs. As he touched her, she felt the moist fabric seep her own fluids against his fingers, and the mental image made her cry out.

"Are you okay?" he asked.

"Yesss," she said, "don't stop, please. Touch me."

He obeyed, moving his hand lower so that he could cup her whole sex with his palm and began to pull upwards in soft gestures, and she lifted her waist toward him with each movement. Nathan dipped his head, trying to inflame all of her nerves, and ran his lips over her stomach, kissing her all over.

Blindly, she groped toward him until her own hand found his member, stiff and rigid against the seams of his pants. *This is crazy*, she thought. It wasn't just that they had only known each other less than a week – *he's a wolf, and I'm a human.* Objectively, it was something she could handle, something her mind could grasp at, however tenuously. But on a subjective level, it was completely different. She reached down and stroked his head, urging him not to stop, and her eyes squeezed tight.

He was moving against her groin quickly, and she felt the tiny pin-pricks in her abdomen and between her legs that signaled an eventual climax. Gently, she coaxed him back to her face and smiled quaintly. Nathan watched her as she shimmied out of her jeans, and then with only a brief moment of shyness pulled her panties down. The stiff curling brush of her pubic hair caught the candlelight, and she moved to cover herself on instinct, but Nathan caught her hand.

"It's okay," he said, and she felt another thrust of her heart as she laid before him. His hands moved back up to her breasts, which peeked out below her bra and T-shirt and laid her back down. He fumbled with the button on his own jeans and pulled them down brusquely.

For him, nudity was not embarrassing. She realized that as a shifter, it was in fact probably more natural for him than for her. Still, she couldn't help but gape at his manhood as he tossed his boxers to one side. The turgid length of it was thick and the bulbous end was ripe with blood.

It was like an animal entirely separate from himself, and she wondered for a moment what his other form looked like. He had never shown it to her, and it seemed like a breach of protocol to ask about it. But now, in his human form, none of that mattered. *I've never felt like this before*, she realized. There was vibrancy to everything, as if the colors had suddenly charged themselves up, and even the small dim glow of the candles seemed to launch the room into brightness.

He kneeled down over her and she gently spread her legs, thrilled by a new sort of vulnerability, one which she was embracing fully with an open heart. Nathan guided his penis toward her vulva, and she winced slightly as it pushed against the moist folds of her labia, but she kept her eyes fixed on his. When he entered her it was like fireworks going off inside her brain, and she let out a long moaning howl as he pressed in further and further.

Nathan's hands came up under her thighs, propping her higher, and he leaned down and kissed her on the mouth as she wrapped her arms around him. He started slowly, easing her into the movement, and she learned to flex and gyrate her hips to accompany his own swelling sex. At first it was painful, and she had to bite her tongue to keep from calling out. But almost as soon as he entered her vagina, she felt her own body react, and something warm pooled against her inner thighs, and she felt it run down the backs of her buttocks.

She groaned again as he sped up, thrusting faster and faster. She opened her mouth to cry out and he buried his face against her neck and squeezed one of her breasts, forcing the elastic of her bra up higher. The skin pressed between his fingers and she lifted her legs up and wrapped them around his naked body as he plunged into her again and again.

“Nathan, don’t stop!” she screamed.

“I’m going to cum,” he murmured, panting into her neck. His buttocks shook with the effort each time he dove against her sex, and she could feel both of their sexes joining in a wet embrace, interlocked together like insects.

“Don’t stop,” she said, groaning, “make me cum.”

Her fingers bit into his neck as he let out a low growl of his own, something that thrummed in his throat like a caught hummingbird, and he made two quick powerful jerks. Both of them were painful, but the second bucked against her G-spot and she quivered, unable to restrain her orgasm. It flowed through her like rain, a pelting hardness, slick and unrelenting and her muscular arms tightened around him as if she would never let him go. Her thighs were on fire as she locked her feet together, holding him deep inside her as he came at the same time. A white light exploded inside her, and all she could do was hold on, even when she felt his seed singe against her insides. She screamed his name again, and bit down hard, grinding her teeth.

Their legs shook and trembled and he picked her up so that she was straddling him upright. Sweat ran down her back as he held her, outlasting her own orgasm that took almost a minute to wind down. She shivered again and her lips were a quivering mass as she childishly sobbed into his shoulder, both breasts flattening their tender pink nipples against his own chest. His hand came down and stroked the small dimples of her lower back as the last vestiges of her orgasm finally left her. Both of their legs were slick, wet with the combined act of lovemaking, and a heavy dark scent filled the bedroom.

The sheets under them were damp, and they both gently careened on their sides, her leg still wrapped over him. Their faces hovered centimeters part, and their foreheads touched as each stroked the other. Nathan's nearly iridescent eyes were full, enacting the very meaning of the word *plenty*, and Nika saw her own reflection.

"Nathan," she said, not wanting to say anything other than his name.

"Yes?"

"Nothing, just that. Nathan."

"You're beautiful on your side like this," he said. "I like the way your hair falls to one side."

She blushed, and ran her fingers over his broad lips, weary but ecstatic with the post-coital flux of endorphins and adrenaline. "You only like my hair?" she asked.

"No," he reached out and touched her eyebrow, then her nose, and finally her lips as well. "I like every part of you. Every part of you is beautiful. Just like this."

"What's going to happen?" Nika asked.

He blinked and rubbed her chin with his thumb. "I don't know. Are you afraid?"

She nodded. "Yes. But I don't know of what. It makes it… harder to be afraid. Maybe that's a good thing, not to see what's coming, so that you can't be afraid of it. What do you think?"

It took him a thoughtful moment to respond. "I think you're right. But I think fear is also important – it keeps us ready, helps us survive."

"Are you afraid?" she queried.

He kissed her on the nose. "Always," he said, "at least a little bit. So, don't be afraid. I'll be afraid for the both of us." She knew in the morning it would sound cheesy, but somehow that quaint compromise put her mind at ease. She closed her eyes and nestled her head against his chest as he pulled the sheets over them, and all she knew as she turned toward the dark door of sleep was his scent.

CHAPTER SIX

Flores let her long prim nails make a *ratatat* sound against the cast iron rim of the bathtub. Since moving to the mansion, she had made herself at home, bringing with her from her own estate on the east coast, everything she could possibly need, including the bathtub. She knew there was a joke in there, but she didn't find it funny.

She had always been fond of the finer things in life. The silk brocades hanging from the wall were Chinese, the elegant four poster bed from France. And only the best wine. She sipped at the dwindling glassful in her long slender hand. *Something from Cheval Blanc*, she wondered, but didn't bother to look at the empty bottle beside the tub.

Looking around her, she felt claustrophobic. She longed for her own estate.

It'd been years since she'd had any face to face contact with the twins, or with her and Dean's reprehensible and senile old father. Of course, Aaron had greeted them both with the sort of obligatory composition of politeness that was expected of him, and while it may have seemed perfectly sentimental to Dean, Flores knew that the old man was only giving them the barest sliver of acceptance. There was too much bad blood on both sides for a true reconciliation. *What do you expect,* she thought, tapping her nails again, *he cut us out of his will and cast us adrift.*

There was more to the story, of course. But only she and Aaron knew the breadth of it. Perhaps that's why he'd suddenly been on edge when all of them had been forced under the same roof again after so many years.

"Dean, get me another bottle," she murmured, sinking back in the tub. Steam floated above, carrying with it the heady scent of herbs. She looked down at herself through the water's mirror. She had always been the skinny awkward child. *Better than being overweight*, she thought. At least this way, a small child-like presence among the other adults, people had a tendency to underestimate her.

"Coming up," Dean said from across the room. He had on a sleeveless dark burgundy T-shirt. His massive biceps cringed and seemed to inflate as he reached for another bottle against the wine-rack in their shared room.

He was a giant of a man, over six feet tall but he had forced himself to hunch the whole time he was here in order not to clip the top of his shaved head. His face was kind, but dumb, the sort of complacent bovine complexion of a beast of burden, a creature with strength to spare, but too simple a mind to know how to use it. It was another family joke that, while the two of them were twins, one of them had gotten the brawn, and one the brains.

"That's my job, dear brother," she said, voicing her

thoughts out loud.

Dean just shrugged. He was used to these non sequiturs from his twin sister.

"You look tense," he observed, and poured her another draught. She sat up as he filled it, and her small breasts, upturned like her nose, flashed their nipples toward the ceiling. "You worried about something? I thought we had this Alpha thing pretty well in the box."

Flores quickly took another drink to quell her rage. Yes, she thought. They had almost convinced the majority of the elders to accept Dean as the new Alpha – sure, there were dissenters, but she knew how to convince them. It only took the proper motivation. But then Aaron had gone and called a public forum. It was a clever strategy, she had to admit, it was also a reminder of where she'd acquired her own surreptitious skill for political strategy.

He's trying to stall this out, she thought.

"Still a ways to go," she replied, gliding back down into the water, "but we'll get there."

"Anything I can do to help?" he asked.

She looked at him, both of his hands hovering over the rim of the bathtub like meaty sausages, his face eager as a dog waiting for a command. *Throw him a bone*, she thought whimsically. "Perhaps, dear brother, perhaps. There are certain things we have to do, preparations that need to be made. You can handle that right?"

Dean stood up and straightened a non-existent collar. Simple minded, maybe, but at least he was ambitious. If he had a sense of his inferiorities, it only made him that much more willing to try and compensate for them. "Whatever you need. What's the plan?"

"We'll be heading to Alaska soon. That's fine… if Aaron wants to drag us north, so be it. But I'm very worried," she said, and pouted out her lower lip. Dean fell for the bait and leaned in.

"What? Why? What's wrong?" he asked, his huge orangutan brow furrowing.

"Safety, Dean. You know that the position of Alpha is dangerous and many people want the leadership. While we were campaigning here, under one roof, it was safe. No one would dare hurt either of us, or Clara or Nathan. We could protect our Pack from outside forces," she said, knowing that Dean would be too one-track to ask *what outside forces*. "But going to Alaska, we'll be unfamiliar territory."

"That's true," he said, stroking his chin. It didn't make him look any brighter, and Flores had to sip at her wine again, almost spilling it into the tub, to keep from smirking. "So what do we do? It can't be canceled, it's Pack writ."

"I know, I know. No, canceling is out of the question. But we can at least make sure that the forum goes according to plan. That means we need protection." Another nod from Dean and she continued, looking pensive, "We might have to call on some outside help."

"You mean the rogue packs?" Dean asked, his voice like an axe being sharpened.

She hid her surprise: he wasn't supposed to get that far ahead. "Perhaps. I know, it sounds dangerous, but with money, enemies can become friends. I think we should… enlist as many warriors as we can."

"That seems dangerous, Flores," he said, standing up. He rubbed the protuberance of his nose absently as if he'd only just discovered it. "They're rogues for a reason. They don't listen to the rest of the Packs. And if anyone from our Pack found out that we'd –"

"Which is why we can't," Flores cut him off with a flippant raise of her hand that splashed water onto the tiles around them. "I know what you're thinking. But father is too narrow-minded about this. We have to keep it a secret. You want to protect us, don't you?"

"Well, of course. I have no ill-will towards Clara or Nathan," he thumped his chest, "but I *am* a better Alpha. The choice is clear. No hard feelings."

"Then you and I will have to go behind our family's back," she motioned him closer with her finger and stroked his pudgy cheek, "in order to save them. Right?"

Her manipulation took a moment to solidify behind his glassy stare, but eventually, it did and Dean nodded. She nodded and gave a tight-lipped smile, another poised and practiced expression that accentuated her demureness. Dean sighed and reached for the bottle of wine but she tapped his hand and made a tut-tut sound with her tongue.

"You get wine, and I don't?" he bristled.

"Wine helps me think," she said, "you don't need to think. I need you to be clear-headed, Dean. Besides, we'd run out of wine trying to get *you* drunk."

He turned with a disappointed and glum look on his face back to a stack of magazines he'd been reading, their laminate covers spread across Flores' bed like a badly assembled collage. She watched his attention sink back into their pages before she filled her glass up again. The noxious breed of wine was sweet, aromatic, and she didn't have to see the label to know it was one of the Aaron's ancient *amarone*.

"He has good taste, at least," she said to herself. "I must have gotten that from him as well."

Dean looked up briefly at her strange slip of vocalization, then back at the pictures in his magazine. Flores always did that, talked out loud, and not to him, but like she was speaking to a ghost or an invisible person. He was used to it.

*

The helicopter thudded heavily as it took off, and before Nika knew it, they were already airborne. She felt her ears pop even through the heavy cushioned clamp of the headphones, and when she dared to look out the window, Calgary was already a diminishing grid of grey streets and buildings. Beside her, Nathan held her hand tightly, and the gesture wasn't missed by Aaron or Clara who sat opposite, though both had the good sense not to point it out.

A second helicopter would come and pick up the other pack members, including Dean and Flores. Nika was thankful for it. After her fateful encounter with Flores, the idea of being near the other shifter filled her with a nameless dread. It was only Nathan's presence that seemed to keep it at bay. But now, as they sailed higher, heading toward a private airport near the rim of the Rocky Mountains, where the landscape abruptly rose from grassy plains into steep sheer granite faces, there was something else to keep her mind occupied.

After having committed so much of her life to a single city, leaving Calgary was both scary and immeasurably exciting, and she was aware of the fact that of the four of them she was the only one wearing a perpetual giddy grin as they soared through the sky.

"First time in a helicopter?" Aaron's voice came through the speakers in her headset.

"Is it that obvious?" she asked, beaming.

"A little," Clara touched her knee. "Look, there's the

landing strip."

It was a small out of the way field, and the attendant on call – the only living person, Nika figured, in probably a hundred kilometers in either direction – was startled by their approach. They could see him fumbling to straighten his hair as the helicopter landed.

"All ready, Earl?" Clara asked, taking the professional lead.

"We got your call, but I didn't really believe it. The plane's all loaded, though, to your specifications," Earl said, and Clara slapped his arm away as he tried several times to salute her, apparently clueless in every respect, but Nika thought he was charming.

"What specifications would those be?" Aaron asked.

He had on a Northface parka the same color as Nika's, but Clara had still opted for her leather jacket. "Never mind that, let's get airborne for now," she barked, never losing a stride as she walked towards the single hangar. The plane inside looked like some sort of prototype, sleek and silver, like a cross between a Lear and a Cessna, just big enough for the four of them.

"Are we waiting for the others, for Flores and Dean, I mean?" Nika asked.

Clara shook her head. "Flores said she had other matters to take care of first," she gave a sickened look. “I don’t know what she’s up to, but she wouldn’t dare miss out on forum. Especially if she wants Dean to assume the Alpha leadership.”

“She’ll follow,” Aaron said wistfully.

“What do you think she’s up to?” Nathan asked. He knew it was an inappropriate question to ask Aaron, especially considering the implications it had in regards to his daughter. But they had gone past being able to tip-toe quietly around family matters.

Nika still hadn’t told him about her meeting with Flores, and she hoped she could keep it a secret between her and Clara. If Nathan knew, he’d probably go after Flores himself; he had enough to worry about. His hand slipped around her waist again, and she leaned gratefully into his shoulder as their footsteps echoed off the hangar.

“I don’t know,” Aaron said at last, “but I can’t believe it’s a coincidence she would take off on some sort of personal business as soon as I called a forum. All we can do is wait and see.”

Behind them, the helicopter lifted off the circular pad, heading back to the city, and Nika wanted to ask who their pilot for the unusual aircraft was before she saw Clara clamber on board, heading for the cockpit. As they strapped in, she had to remark on the opulence of it; it was like flying in a mini limousine.

“You think that’s fancy,” Nathan said, and pressed one of the buttons on the table that they were sharing.

The smell of fine leather and air freshener filled the cabin, and there was a slight swishing sound as the main counter folded back to reveal a chilled selection of wine and glasses. "One for you, Aaron?"

He held up a hand. "No, never on flights. I get queasy enough as it is."

Nathan shrugged and poured a glass for himself and Nika and held it up. In the other cabin, they heard Clara fiddling with buttons and starting up the pre-engine sequence, followed by an invective locution of swear words.

"Is she… going to be alright in there?" Nika asked.

"Welcome to the ship of fools," Aaron said, tucking his hands into his armpits and trying to close his eyes.

"She's got her license," Nathan said. "Here's to us not falling out of the sky." Nika wrinkled her nose at the joke, and wondered how much of it was really a jest as the plane lurched forward, picking up speed. Nathan reached out again to touch her hand. "It's okay. Everything will be okay," he said.

"Is that a promise?"

He tilted his head and blinked against the sun as it wound its way through the window and the plane soared over the mountains, heading northwest. He nodded. "Promise."

The flight passed without incident, and the next thing

Nika knew, they were circling above a dark green expanse on one side, and a chilly blue expanse on the other, and she realized it was the ocean. She'd been to the coast a number of times in her childhood, but from this height she could finally get a solid grasp of just how large it was. The Pacific stretched north to south and then west into an infinite regress against the horizon.

There was no evidence of buildings or structures, or human life at all. The Alaskan wilderness was flush below them, and she felt a kind of inverse vertigo as she looked out the window until she sat back down. Aaron was awake again, but muttering under his breath about planes and how people were better off using their own legs.

"We're there already?" she asked.

"You've been asleep for hours," Nathan said, his black locks catching over his forehead. "That's Anchorage down there." There was a small faint white outline in the distance against one of the shores, and smoke coming from several places, but even from up high it could have been mistaken for a forest fire.

"That's where we're going?"

"No, Anchorage is a human settlement. Where we're going… a human hasn't stepped foot for centuries. You'll be the first in a very long time." He adjusted his seatbelt, and rapped his knuckle against the cabin door to the cockpit to signal Clara.

"You mean the ancestral lands… wherever that is," Nika whispered.

"Aye, lass," Aaron said, opening one eye.

They flew for another twenty minutes, and before Nika knew it they were descending again, but toward what looked like the canopy of the forest. Clara's expert maneuvering took them into a smooth arc that leveled out, and the tops of pine and spruce flashed by outside the window. Then she saw they were actually heading for a meadow – no, rather something that had been disguised to look like a meadow. The tires of the plane hit asphalt which had been painted over and then carefully covered with a thin assemblage of twigs and branches and moss. In the distance, emerging from the tree line, were a number of shapes, but it was hard to discern what they were.

As the four of them descended the stairs onto the ground, Nika tucked in beside Nathan who put an arm around her. The figures were closer now, and she could see them in all their glory – some were human, men and women in average looking clothing, but there were beasts among them, huge dire wolves that loped beside the humans, their hackles raised.

"Nathan," she murmured.

"It's alright," he replied. "That's Corin. He leads the northern pack here."

Corin led the procession as they came out of the woods, and he had on a long black sweater up to his neck. His features were etched and eroded, but there was the same gentleness in his eyes that belonged to Aaron. His skin was almost ochre, and when he smiled, his cheeks pulled far back up his face. He greeted them all in kind, and then stopped when he got to Nika.

"Hello," he said in a deep voice, reminiscent of the earth moving under their feet, "it's not often we welcome a human into our midst. You are most welcome." She gave a nod as he turned to Aaron and both men locked arms. "And you, clan brother, it's been a long time. City life has made you fat."

Corin bellowed out a laugh, and Aaron winced. "Speak for yourself."

The clan leader was still smiling as he patted his old friend on the back. "There will be plenty of time to speak of many things. Let's get out of the open, though. There's a feast in the village tonight and I think we have other things to speak of," he said.

Nika looked back and saw that several of the men and women were busy pushing the plane off the hidden runway, and several of the dire-wolves had tethers strapped to their collars, or gnashed tightly between their teeth, and were pulling with equal force. *Efficient*, she observed, *and well organized.* It gave her hope that perhaps whoever was behind her attack would be dissuaded from trying to start anything here. *Still, Clara said she doesn't know how deep it goes.*

Her hand tightened on Nathan's and he turned, but

she shook her head. Could it be that Flores really wanted power so badly? And if not Flores, then who else? *No, it has to be her*, Nika grimaced, remembering how she'd been shamelessly thrown onto the bed naked, the lingering perverted stare the shifter had given her.

The small party followed Corin in a procession, and she could feel the curious glances of other shifters, both human and wolf, glancing across the unusual human in their midst. She didn't sense any hostility, only curiosity. Once she tried to catch the gaze of a large grey dire wolf stepping lightly through the ferns to their right, and smiled at it; it jerked backwards as if struck, and then hacked loudly, trying to hide its own embarrassment at being unnerved.

"Many of Corin's people haven't seen a human in years," Clara said gently over her shoulder, "They live out here in the sacred lands. Like mine and Nathan's parents, Corin is the guardian of something too, you might think of him like a custodian."

By time they reached Corin's village, it was near evening, but still light enough to see between the trees. They'd been walking for what seemed hours, and Nika rubbed her thighs as they made it to the last hill and stared down the gulley at another cloistered meadow. There were a number of huts arranged in a semi-circle, and the smell of smoke and wood and meat drifting upwards. She barely had time to register it before they were ushered down the slope. In the village, there were more than just wolves and men and women – children in second-hand clothes, or some none at all, ran to get a look at the newcomers.

Nika smiled shyly as they huddled around her knees, pulling on her pant leg and looking up at her with huge round eyes and laughing. Corin shooed them away and led the four of them to one of the bigger huts. The longhouse was very traditional, and the smell of open cedar wood was sweet and enveloping, and made Nika a little dizzy as they entered the darkness within which was heavy with residual smoke.

Two of the long haired men who'd been at the reception closed the doors, and it took a minute for all of their eyes to adjust. Corin, in his unassuming way, took a seat on the wooden slatted floor on one side of an open fire pit. He narrowed his lips and blew into the basin, and the red eyes of coals blazed to life. Clara, Nathan, and Aaron both sat down cross-legged as well, and Nika joined them.

"Aaron has told me about your suspicions," Corin said at last, facing them all, "but frankly, I can't believe it. The idea that someone else in the Pack would harm another like this, it's unspeakable and goes against every way we've ever held."

"I know it's painful to consider, Corin, but we can't afford to take risks this time," Aaron offered.

"And what about you, old friend? You suspect someone?" Both Nathan and Clara lowered their heads, and Nika again felt the old wolf's pain bubble to the surface as he sat there. He seemed older, now.

A great weight had perched itself on either shoulder. Corin must have noticed as well because he opened his mouth in an *ah* shape and said no more.

"You are one of the only other elders who knows about the transgenic gene," Aaron whispered, all of the energy of his usual self seemingly drained, dampened by an irrepressible sadness, "but it is possible that Flores may have discovered the secret as well. Clara is extremely resourceful to have found out on her own, but you'll pardon me if I give Flores more credit when it comes to poking her nose in places it doesn't belong."

"Still no proof," Clara said, trying to entice hope into the old man.

"No, and there may never be. But at least here during forum all three of you will be safe," Aaron waved a hand at Nika and the two siblings, "and we can get this rite of leadership over once and for all. All the other elders and pack leaders are in agreement?"

Nika nudged Nathan for clarification. "The rite of leadership involves a number of elements," he whispered, "but at heart, we're still wolves – still tied to old ways – which means a ritual combat will be the final test. Between me and Dean."

She felt a stab of fear. She had never met the other Alpha candidate in person, but she'd seen him more than once wandering around the gardens and estates. He had given her curt smiles and nods, and little more, but like the other shifters here in the village, she had sensed no outward hostility, not like Flores. But he was definitely a monster in terms of sheer size. She had actually gaped the first time she saw him moving through the house, each footstep rocking the plates on their shelves.

Nathan is strong, but against an opponent like that, what chance does he stand? she thought, and her lower lip curled under her teeth again. Beside her, Clara reached out again and her steely fingers settled over Nika's having read the other woman's body language.

"Some have arrived already," Corin continued, "others will continue to arrive until tomorrow morning. They have all heard the call of forum. What of Flores and Dean? They didn't come with you?"

"No," Aaron said nervously, "but they will come. I have no doubt of that."

"I see," Corin said. The gravity in his voice was tectonic, a force that belonged to the deep places of the earth, immovable in its certainty of plain facts and what it saw with its own eyes. "For now, we keep this a secret," he said, his eyes landing on Nika. "The attack on you should not be brought to light. Unfortunately, your Pack already knows the details, Nathan, but the less the others know about it, the smoother the forum will proceed."

"Agreed," Nathan said. "Although on the other hand, if we publicly announced what had happened, it might flush our conspirator into the light."

“Or it could scare them away for good, or worse, force their hand in a way we can’t predict.” Clara bit her thumb. “No, Corin’s right. For now, we’ll keep it a secret. Let the forum continue without interruption. I think patience is probably the best weapon at our disposal right now.”

Outside, there were cheers from the village as another cohort of shifters arrived, and Corin rubbed his brow and tossed the long wispy strands of his greying hair over one shoulder. “Unfortunately, that doesn’t excuse me from my duties as chief – time to greet the others,” he said. “What is you told me once, Aaron… the simplest form of diplomacy is a smile?” He flashed a huge row of yellowing teeth.

CHAPTER SEVEN

The feast was aptly named. As night descended and the stars prickled into existence above the tops of the trees, several huge bonfires were lit. Nika found it hard to venture a guess at just how many shifters had actually convened, but she figured it was at least several hundred. Laughter and loud voices caroused through the air, and she found herself at Nathan's side again near one of the largest bonfires. The crackling of it was like bones being broken under the jaws of wolves. Several of the dire wolves had managed to worm their way among the other dancing bodies, and Nathan told her that for some shifters, there was a preference, either for the wolf or human shape.

One of the younger wolves, a smaller pup with a grey streak down his back and black paws, nestled up close to her where she was sitting on a crude tiered bench and table. It nuzzled against her, seemingly ignorant of the fact she was human, and she tentatively scratched behind his ears.

"His name is Aiden," Nathan said, handing her a wooden bowl with meat on it.

She ate with her hands, surprised at her own gluttonous appetite. This was the complete opposite of the life she had had in Calgary. There she was used to restaurants, take away, Chinese food. Here, under the stars, scarfing down venison among a horde of smiling and laughing shifters, she felt more alive than she'd ever felt, and burst into her own high pitched laughter.

Hot greasy fat ran down her chin, and Nathan grinned rubbing his finger under her mouth to catch the drops. *I'm not one of them*, she thought, *and yet they treat me as if I were*. Even Aaron, who had become disparagingly grumpy in the last few days, managed to brighten up as fresh homemade wine was handed around the orange pyre in a leather flask. When it was Nika's turn, several of the other women coaxed her gently, and Nathan raised his shoulders helplessly.

"How was it?" he asked, after she'd taken her fair share.

She wiped her mouth with the back of her hand. "Better than a daiquiri," she said, and when he gave her a befuddled look she burst into laughter again and leaned her head against his chest.

The feast continued unabated for hours, and Nika was able to gauge it from the progress of the half-moon as it wended its way across the heavens. Daybreak was still several hours away, and she rolled on her side and nuzzled closer to Nathan who was asleep. He absently wrapped his arm around her, stroking the back of her head. The last remains of the fires were only smoking embers now, laid to waste by ashes. Everyone was asleep, sprawled on the ground or benches, or curled on their own sleeping mats, humans and wolves alike buried against one another.

Nika smiled, glimpsing the whole community like this, each of them with a placid smile on their lips, the simple happiness that touch brought, a knowledge so innately obvious that you belonged somewhere. *I want that*, she thought. As a human, could she ever truly belong among these people? Yes, they were abiding, kind, unerringly welcoming. But to *belong*, that was a hard thing.

She considered closing her eyes again, but a dark movement near the tree line caught her attention, and she raised her head sleepily; another movement, swift. She tried to clear the cobwebs of the homemade wine and sat straight up. One of the shapes stopped abruptly, higher up on a hill and occluded by the dark trunks of several old growth cedars, and she got a good look at it.

Four legged and massive, but gaunt as if half-starved. Another dire wolf, except this one had odd metal braces on his legs, a strange iron-wrought armor that wound up over its muzzle and across its flanks. Straddling its back, another figure, human, except he was dressed in an odd assortment of patch-work leather and canvas, and he had a long tattered cloak with a hood pulled high up. It wasn't until he turned, and Nika saw his face, that she screamed.

A crude wooden mask covered his features, rough hewn to look vaguely like a face. But the eyes that blazed out from behind it through narrow openings were unmistakably the eyes of a killer, someone who had seen plenty of it. As Nika screamed, something black whizzed past her face, scratching her cheek, and she ducked as another arrow whistled into the hard tier of the make-shift throne behind her.

Nathan's eyes flashed open at the same time and he sat up just in time to see another flurry of arrows. He grabbed Nika and rolled on top of her, two of the black shafts striking into the hard packed ground where they'd been lying.

"Attack! We're under attack!" another voice bellowed, and Nika looked up and saw Corin standing tall and lifting a simple wooden mallet.

All around, the villagers and pack members struggled awake, surprise turning into panic. More of the staggered shapes lunged around the tree line, keeping themselves hidden and surrounding the entire enclosure. Black arrows hissed through the air, clotting it with their barbs, and several screams issued from those who had been struck. Nika gasped as Nathan lifted her up by the arm and they ran towards one of the longhouses. One of the young women who had helped her to the homemade wine earlier that night fell backwards with a stunned look as an arrow caught her in the breast.

Nathan swore, and somehow they made it to Corin's side. Several of the villagers had huddled together, using benches as shields. "Corin! What's going on?!" Nathan shouted, and pulled Nika down as another arrow sailed over her head. "Where's Clara… Aaron?"

The old leader shook his head. "I don't know," he said, "We can't stay in the open like this, we have to try to break through. Go, Nathan, to the longhouse… the cubs are there. We have to get them out of here."

Several riders came out of the woods, and Nathan snarled. Their wolves were smaller, but there was a feral quality to them that bordered on rabid. The cloaked and masked riders both were armed with bows and two quivers each crisscrossing on their backs. More arrows struck, one of them finding its way between the shields, and the man next to Nika screamed as a black shaft grew out of his eye. He struggled for a minute, and then was still, his good eye fixed toward the bluish tinge of sky. Nika felt sick and held her mouth.

"We're betrayed," Corin spat. "Move! Don't let them come any closer!" He shouted at his own villagers, many who had now regained their senses and were holding off the circling attacks. "Please, Nathan, go… protect the little ones," he begged, his bronzed face stricken with fear for the safety of those he had sworn to protect.

"What about you?!"

"I'm the chief of this village," Corin managed to summon an uneven smile. "I don't know how this is going to end Nathan, but I know you also have what it takes to be a chief. You remember, what your father said – about the true mark of leadership?"

Nathan's hands curled up like snail-shells into tight bloodless fists. "We die for the ones we love." It was barely a whisper, and Nika wasn't sure if he'd spoken at all.

"Aye. Now go!" Corin barked, and grabbed an arrow

out of the air, breaking it cleanly between his fingers. Several of the villagers had turned into wolves and were trying out flank the raiders and lure them away.

Nika nodded at Nathan.

They waited for the next volley of arrows and took off at a run, side by side. Several arrows flew by their heads, but they could only focus on getting to the longhouse. Nika's boots slid on the mud and she righted herself just as two more riders leapt out of the bushes to their right. Nathan dove towards one of the broken fences used to hedge the pigs that the village raised and pulled one of the heavy stakes out of the ground. The rider made a sound like a laugh behind his mask as he leapt off his wolf. The wolf snarled and advanced on Nathan who pushed the sharp spear towards the creature.

The rider watched for a moment and then turned toward Nika who had frozen again. His black eyes blinked and he reached up and pulled the mask off. She almost screamed again when she recognized the scarred face of the man who had attacked her in the park.

"Time to settle up, miss," he said, and ran towards her with a whooping yell.

She moved her right foot back in the mud, anchoring her posture. She had been taken by surprise the first time, but too much had happened since then for her to be so easily startled. The shifter swung out at her with his bow and she lifted her forearm and knee to block.

A sharp sting slapped through her jeans and the cuff of her sweater, and she spun around.

All the practice at Tae Kwon Do paid off – she felt her foot connect with the man's ear and he huffed and landed in the mud, livid with rage. He slapped the ground and pounced toward her again. This time, she didn't have the advantage, and his own hands gripped her shoulders like talons. She felt her foot give out under her as they both fell backwards, and the muddy ground nearly knocked the wind out of her.

Not like this, she thought, trying to maintain the speed of his attack as she pulled her knees up under her and kicked upwards. The man gave a surprised squeal as he sailed over her, landing hard on the ground behind. Nika was up in an instant, her posture ready for a second attack. Mud caked her pants and back, and was streaked on her face and in her hair.

"Bitch!" he screamed, and sprinted toward her, his scarred face possessed by pain and wounded pride.

He was acting in anger, and Nika knew she had regained the high ground. She acted as if to block his attack, and then swiveled on her foot again, bringing her leg around in a sweeping arc that tripped him. He plummeted face first into the mud and swore savagely again. This time, he reached under the soiled folds of his cloak, and she saw steel glint in the new dawn, the same sort of dagger he'd used once before to slice her. She gulped, looking around for a weapon, even as his feet splashed through the mud toward her.

As if by magic, he suddenly flew backwards, and let out a groan, and it took half a heartbeat for her to notice the muddy wooden stake protruding from his belly. His fingers clutched at the ground in a futile attempt to hold onto whatever life was left, and then he was still. She turned around, gasping for air, and Nathan lowered his arms. Next to him a crumpled furred shape rested in a growing pool of its own blood, mingling with the dirt until they were both the same color.

"Let's go," Nathan breathed. He was equally muddy, and his shirt was torn open on one side where two parallel cuts oozed bright red. His jaw had become an iron vice again, and his eyes were furious as a bird of prey.

At the entrance of the longhouse, Nika kicked the door in, and suddenly felt something sharp against her throat. Like a ghost, Clara emerged from the shadows, and lowered a hunting knife.

"Geezus, I thought you were one of them," Clara said, and Nathan guarded their retreat inside, "When the attack happened I came here." She pointed behind her at two dozen youngsters, all of them crouched and quiet. They'd been trained from a young age to recognize danger, and to rely on the adults to protect them. Now they waited, patiently.

"We have to get them out of here," Nathan said. "I don't know how long Corin can hold them off. We aren't safe in here, though. If they decide to light their arrows up, we'll be caught in an oven."

“Who *are* they?” Clara said, picking up one of the smallest children, a young girl whose doe-like eyes fastened on Nika and never moved.

Nathan shook his head, and Nika stooped to comfort another of the younger boys who had cut his knee in an attempt to run to the safety of the longhouse. “One of them,” Nika said, “one of them I recognized from the park. It’s the same guy.”

“So we are betrayed,” Clara’s anger was palpable.

“There’s a back entrance, right?” Nathan said, striding across the floor of the longhouse. “We’ll head into the woods, try to lose them. C’mon.”

“They’ll catch up with us,” Clara shook her head. “At least here we have some defense. Out there, it’s too easy for them to pick us off.”

“No, I have an idea,” Nathan said, “but we have to move… now!”

Both women looked at each other, intimidated by the sudden urgency in Nathan’s voice. He had just killed a shifter, one of his own kind, but there was no time to regret. Survival had overtaken all of his senses – that and a self-same duty, like Corin, to protect those who couldn’t protect themselves. Nika nodded and picked up the young boy, hurrying the other children after him with Clara taking up the rear.

At the back of the longhouse, they paused for a moment. The rout was still continuing, and there were loud shouts and screams. Another flurry of arrows from the tree line arced down toward where Corin and the others were making a stand. *I hate to leave them*, Nathan thought. Whoever these raiders were, they were fast, well organized and they'd waited until the opportune moment to strike. He winced when he saw the bodies of the villagers littering the ground.

"Easy, little brother, we have our task," Clara comforted, catching up and tapping his shoulder.

He nodded and snuck toward the base of the trees, urging the line of children after him. They obeyed noiselessly. Nathan crept slowly into the deeper bush, trying to choose places that had high ferns where they could hide themselves. Behind them, the cries of wolves and warriors alike began to diminish, but Nika knew they were still far from being safe.

After almost fifteen minutes of scrambling on hands and knees, they made it to a small ravine that led down toward a creek. Some of the older children helped to lower the younger, and Nika found herself beside a youth in his teens.

"That's all of them," he replied, his voice high and almost feminine.

"Do I know you?" Nika asked suddenly.

He smiled. "Aiden," he replied, and Nika remembered the wolf pup that curled up beside her affectionately the night before. She put a hand to her mouth – *they're all so young*, she thought.

"Here," Nathan said, when Clara had made it to the bottom. The young girl was clinging to her back now, silent as a mouse. "This creek will throw off their scent. You head downriver, Clara. Keep them safe. I don't know how far it is, but it should meet one of the bigger rivers. You should be able to avoid any raiders."

Clara clenched her fists. "What do you mean? You're not going back there!" she spat.

"No," he said, and this time it was his turn to tap her shoulder. "You were right, it's easy to pick us off out here. If Corin can't hold off the raiders, they'll be coming for the children next. Can't let that happen. I'll stay here, back up the path, and lead them away in the other direction. Upstream."

"You can't," Clara insisted.

The children were all gathered, and looked up at her expectantly – the only chance they had rested in the older woman's vigilance and determination, and Clara knew it. But to leave her own brother behind was an almost unbearable loss.

"You and Nika need to protect the children," he said. "Please. I'll be alright. Fuckers won't be able to catch me, but I'll be plenty damned if I let them hurt any of these young 'uns. Now, go. Go, Clara."

Clara sniffed and wrapped her arms around Nathan. He hugged her back, and didn't try to look her in the face as she turned. There were tears she didn't want him to see, tears that would make it too difficult to continue if he saw.

"I'm staying, too," Nika said all of a sudden. Both shifters looked at her. "Don't try and argue. I can be of more use if I try to lure them away with Nathan. I'm a human, remember. If I go with the children, it'll be a cinch for the raiders to pick up on my scent. Nathan and I can lure them away, I know we can."

Clara gulped. The burden of her responsibility had shifted against her will. She merely gave a nod and headed downstream without another word. The children looked at Nathan and Nika once, and then followed after Clara, their soft footsteps eaten up by the roar of water.

"Nika," he murmured.

"We have to work to do," she said, cutting him off.

He looked back up the ravine, and shook his head. "If they come, we'll be overrun in seconds," he turned and looked her over and clicked his tongue, "unless we find a faster pair of legs for you." He gave a little chortle and stepped to one side of the creek, tearing the dirty ripped shirt off his chest.

"What are you—" Nika was about to say.

"You need a wolf to fight wolves," he said. "Guess it's about time you saw what I really am."

He took off his pants and boxers as well, and stood

muddy and naked before her. She fought back a latent feeling of desire and watched as he crouched on all fours and lowered his head. His lean muscles flexed against their caked mask of mud, and he grunted. She felt another surge of desire, remembering the same ejaculation of sound when they had made love.

In moments, his body began to tremble, and she tried to restrain her surprise as fur began to bleed out from his limbs and his face contorted outwards, lengthening into a snarling muzzle. In moments, a huge black wolf was squatting where Nathan had once been, and even though she knew instinctively it was *still* Nathan, the difference in forms was almost too hard to comprehend.

He made a barking sound and she came forward, putting a hand on his head, and shyly clambered onto his back. He made another barking sound of satisfaction and began to walk forward. She dug her heels into his side to hold on, and wrapped her hands into fists around the fur of his collar as he leapt across the bank and backtracked up the steep slope.

"I'm scared, Nathan," she admitted into the wolf's black ears.

He ducked his head and let out a guttural growl. *So am I.*

For long moments they waited, both of them balanced on the silence of the forest, the small inner mechanisms of nature going about their business, the quotidian functions of the wilderness. After several minutes, Nathan's ears pricked up, and Nika tightened her grip on his fur. There were howls, some human and some wolf. *Go, let's go*, she wanted to say, but Nathan remained fixed, statue-like. *He's trying to lure them in as close as possible, to make sure they see us for sure,* she realized. Whatever lead they could give Clara and the children, it was up to them now.

Three raiders broke into the clearing and froze, suddenly face to face with a full-fledged dire wolf. On his back, Nika glowered at the wooden masked attackers who all calmly nocked more black arrows into their bows. A tense moment seemed to generate out of a collective fury, and then snapped all at once.

"Run!" Nika shouted.

Nathan took off at a sprint, so fast she almost fell off and caught her breath as she ducked low. An arrow slammed into a tree trunk beside them, and there were shouts of surprise from behind as the raiders took up the chase. Ferns and undergrowth flashed by in a blur of green as Nathan headed toward the creek and then broke right, heading upstream. Nika looked behind and felt relief when she saw the raiders blindly take after them. *Clara will be safe*, she thought.

But that still didn't bode well for them. Another arrow glanced off a stone beside them. Nathan was running full on now, his muzzle slavering with drool as he pushed his body to the limit, scattering branches and stones under his paws. Nika could feel his heartbeat slamming through his ribs as the wind whipped past both of them.

Towards their left, she saw the cliff rising in a sharp face, and tapped Nathan's collar. His lupine eyes glanced it and he aimed toward the dusty slopes, panting as he worked his way up the switchbacks. Behind them, the three raiders were gaining. *One chance,* Nika thought, and she hoped that Nathan had seen it and understood.

When they reached the top Nathan turned around and Nika hopped off. The ridge was skinny. On one bank, the raiders were clambering up towards them, on the other it dipped off sharply into a perilous fall below. Nika nodded at Nathan, and he slinked backwards, taking cover behind one of the giant boulders. When the raiders came up, they'd see the human first. *And if we're lucky, that's all the surprise we'll need*, she thought.

She waited. Another arrow flew wildly upwards, skidding against the bank. *Wait.*

The first two raiders reached the top and snarled when they saw their prey. Nika spat at them and threw a stone towards them, which ricocheted uselessly off the chest of one. The raiders snarled again and leapt towards her, the riders eager to let their mounts taste human blood.

Jaws snapped a foot from her face, and Nika didn't blink. From behind the boulder, Nathan lunged at both, body-checking both wolves against one another. There was a whine of pain as the first one clipped into his companion, and paws scrambled for purchase on the slippery ridge. Nathan lunged again, using his front paws to push outward.

Both raiders and their wolves screamed as they toppled over the backside of the ridge, and Nika winced when she heard the crack of bones and dislocation of muscles and joints. A huge storm of dust kicked up as the four bodies rolled down the cliff, finally stopping at the base of another creek. There was no time to congratulate themselves, however, as the third raider appeared behind.

Nathan went to meet the wolf's jaws, acting as a shield for Nika. The attacker's teeth crunched into Nathan's shoulders and he howled and swung his own head against the wolf's like a hammer. At the same time, Nika rolled to one side and clutched at a black bow that had fallen from the grip of the other raider. There was a single arrow at her foot and she nocked it and let it fly in the space of one breath.

Nothing happened for a moment, and she was certain she had missed.

Then, slowly, the raider on top of the wolf slid to one side, his hood coming down and his mask topping off his face as he hit the ground. A small barb was lodged in his throat, and his right hand clutched at the wound in disbelief. His wolf companion, alarmed by the death of its rider, turned in shock and anger at the human.

"Nathan, help," she pleaded, holding the bow in front

of her.

The black wolf shook his head, his arm still aching, and made a final lunge at the other shifter. They scrambled for a moment, and Nathan kicked out with his hind legs. The other shifter seemed to balance in mid-air for a moment, and then opened its mouth in a long whine as it fell backwards, its legs scraping at the empty air.

It hit a rise in the switchbacks below and bounced, severing its spine, and fell the rest of the way down the slope like a ragdoll until the net of trees and branches finally stopped it. Nika, on her belly, looked over the edge, her lungs burning. Beside her, Nathan let out a whimpering sigh and she saw him change back, his black fur scattering about him like leaves, until he was human again. There were puncture marks in his shoulder, deep, but not fatal.

“Ow,” he murmured. “Are you okay, Nika?”

She looked over the edge again. “Fine,” she murmured. “Just fine.”

*

A half kilometer down the ridge, they found a small cave bored into the side of the granite cliff, and Nika helped him squirm into the back into it. An animal must have used it in the past because the floor was lined with a soft layer of moss that was spongy under Nathan’s naked feet. She set him down and he hissed, clutching his side.

“I’ll be right back,” she whispered and was gone again before he could stop her.

She returned several minutes later barefoot and both her boots filled with water from the creek. Her own skin was gleaming and wet and her hair was damp and clean again as well, and she poured the ice cold salve against his skin and wounds. Exhausted, he let out a cough and examined the bite in his shoulder.

“Flesh wound,” he said. “I don’t think that wolf really knew what to do with his jaws.”

“Still looks painful,” Nika said, crouching down beside him.

“My regenerative abilities will take care of it. Nothing to fear,” he said, trying to sound upbeat. In the dim light, the contours of his body seemed to transform him into another element of the cave. Nika started shaking, and clutched her own shoulders.

“Are you hurt?” he asked reaching forward.

“No, just…” she couldn’t finish her sentence.

Nathan sat up and wrapped his arms around her, enfolding her in an embrace, and his hand stroked her head. Her clothes were soaked and grimy, and where she’d washed herself in the creek her skin rose upward in tiny goose bumps. She sighed when he touched her and her forehead pressed against his chest.

“We did it,” he whispered. “Clara and the kids are going to be okay. And we’re okay, too, right? Look at me.” He touched her chin and raised it toward his face. His eyes luminesced again, fracturing whatever light existed around them and crystallizing it.

Nika pushed herself forward and kissed him, and he opened his eyes in surprise. She closed her own, kissing him harder, wanting nothing more than to be held. The images of the slaughter at the village ran across her mind, the screams and the blood and the fear, especially of the scar-faced shifter, the one who had haunted her dreams for weeks. Sobs began to quake her body and Nathan pulled her back, brushing the hair out of her face, and kissed her forehead and her cheeks and her eyelids.

“Nathan,” she mouthed.

He shook his head and she sniffed and kissed him again. Her fingers undid the damp buttons on her shirt and the wet tangle of it peeled off her white skin. She knew it was only an escape, a way to hide from the pain and confusion, but she also knew that it could only be Nathan; the one who had saved her on more than one occasion, the only one in the world she wanted to be beside.

Nika’s fingers undid the strap on her bra and it came away lightly. Both her breasts were round, smooth in the dim light. Her nipples were already hard from the cold water, but she let out a pleasurable sigh as his hands pushed against her chest, kneading them in small circles. She let him suck her neck as she fiddled with the buttons on her jeans and unzipped them, and Nathan helped her out of them. She hesitated only for a moment taking her panties off, and then she was as naked as the first time they had made love.

Nika pushed him back down on the moss and threw one leg over top of him. When she looked down, she saw he was already stiffening in anticipation, his member throbbing with the left-over adrenaline of the chase. She moved down and took it in one hand, squeezing and feeling it harden more, swelling against her fingers like something trying to escape. Timidly, she placed her lips over top of it and rubbed her tongue against the bulb. Nathan stiffened and leaned back, closing his eyes as she pleasured him, and she looked up from her work and sucked harder, forcing his member to the back of her throat.

"Oh, god," he murmured, his legs twitching.

Her effect on him only heightened her pleasure, and she began to dip and lower her mouth against his penis, and felt a sickly sweet flavor permeate her cheeks as she pulled it out again with a gasp. Her saliva glistened against the shaft and she scooted up again, and perched above him.

"Fuck me," she whispered, leading his sex towards hers.

She reached down and touched her own genitals, found them warm and moist, and spread her vagina with two fingers so that he could get a better look. The pink folds peeled back as she pulled his cock into her and both of them let out a simultaneous groan. She straddled him again, lowering herself further, and the dark wet cavern of her groin accepted him fully as she arched her back. Her breasts swayed outward as Nathan continued to fondle them, and his hands moved lower, grasping her ribs and the broad rims of her hips as she grinded into him.

“Unhhh, yes,” she murmured, “like that.”

Nathan’s abdominal muscles clenched and unclenched as he lifted his own hips into hers until the two of them found a perfect fluid movement. Nika let out a little cry and pushed her hand between her legs and felt a warm gush of her first orgasm seep between her fingers. The curled mass of her pubic hair scraped against his as she worked herself harder and harder.

She reached behind and put her hands on his knees for support as she opened her thighs wider and thrust harder. His member swelled inside her, rubbing against her insides with such intensity she had to bite her lip again to keep from crying out. She huffed and leaned over him, her hair brushing against his face and falling around it so that the two of them were looking up through a tunnel of it at each other’s groaning faces.

“Harder, almost... almost there,” she said, “ohhhh, god, Nathan.”

“I love you, Nika,” he whispered and hugged her tightly, pounding himself upwards until she screamed and moaned into his ear and his other hand came down, spreading over her buttocks. They came at the same time again, and Nika made a growling sound as he ejaculated against her, pulling out just in time to smear his seed against her pubic hair and stomach.

Her climax was equally potent, and once again she sobbed as a trembling overtook her and Nathan held her against him. Her legs quivered against his, rocking against her will as her nervous system overloaded itself.

"Ahhh, Nathan, hold me, unnh," she moaned, her lips wet and open and searching for his own. His tongue found hers and he embraced her, still clutching her sweating body against his own until she finally gave an ultimate sigh and relaxed against him, her breath hot and heavy on his neck, and her lips still brushing against his skin.

He rolled her off of him and wrapped both arms around her as they spooned, her own lithe buttocks fitting into the socket of his crotch, and she counted her breaths. The smells of the cave seemed to create its own atmosphere, something that was subterranean and wholly primeval, and she felt as if she'd climbed out of her own skin, as if somehow she had managed to slough off her own humanity, and become something *other*.

Nathan's face buried against the back of her head and he stroked her face. She took his hand around her belly and moved it up until his arm was across her breasts, and she wound her own fingers between his.

She wanted to feel safe, even if she knew that it was an illusion.

Neither of us are safe, she thought.

"Nathan," she said at last.

"Yes," he replied.

"I'm not scared," she said, and realized how childish it sounded.

He squeezed her again, trying to fold himself around her. "I know," he said, "I know."

"What are we going to do?"

For several minutes, Nathan didn't say anything, and she wondered if he'd simply gone to sleep but at last his voice broke, gravelly and resolute. "We need to head back," he said, starting out the cave entrance. "If Corin and the others survived, we'll try to meet up with them. Then, I don't know."

"I didn't see… Aaron," she said in a shushed tone.

He shook his head. "Nor I. But the old wolf's survived much worse."

She squirmed against him and turned around so she could face him. "Flores wasn't there. I didn't see her," she said, and Nathan nodded. "Do you think…?"

"I don't know, Nika," he said, "but I aim to find out."

She nodded and tucked her head against his chest again. Outside, they waited while the sun slowly declined, painting its orange glow across the forest. Names and faces gathered in her mind, and she gave each an equal amount of time before she moved to the next. Aaron, Corin, Flores, Dean, James. And Nathan.

Tomorrow would mean facing death again – the raiders and the wolves. Her heart jumped a beat thinking about it, but Nathan reached out and drew her toward him. There was no need for language, no need for anything but this.

Tomorrow may never come, she thought.

"I love you, too," she whispered, closing her eyes.

CHAPTER EIGHT

Flores looked dejectedly out the window of the helicopter. Dawn was just breaking over the horizon to the west, and there was that liminal light that was halfway between its phases, half formed. The steady thumping of the rotors for the past hour and a half had started to give her a migraine, and she rubbed her temples, trying to think clearly through the heavy droning haze. Her brother Dean was silent beside her. His huge bulky form, attired in a nylon jacket, seemed enraptured by the landscape unfolding under them like a dark green mat. Huge mountains to the west were starting to take shape, and further north, Flores knew the Denali Range lifted upwards, the highest point on the continent.

They weren't going that far. After landing in Anchorage, the helicopter had picked them up without delay. She was starting to feel the weariness of travel, even though she'd mostly been sitting for the past twelve hours, she could feel a strange sort of exhaustion coming over her. By now, the forum had already been called, and the other packs would have been assembled. She gnawed on her lower lip and folded her hands in her lap and her sharp nails began to dig into the flesh of her knuckles.

For the last three months, the new leadership of their Pack – the position of Alpha – had been up in the air, split between her twin brother Dean and their cousin Nathan. *Nathan*, she scowled, picturing the handsome and delicate features of the young man. In her youth, she had a crush on him, but it was something she had never admitted to anyone, least of all to herself. She knew that as far as qualities went, he was a worthy contestant for the election, someone who stood a good chance. *But if he manages to snare the Alpha position instead of Dean*, she thought, *then the two of us will be relegated to a lower tier.* Her power would be symbolic, lip service.

"Can't let that happen," she said aloud.

Dean turned at her outburst, and then looked back out the window with a bored expression. His sister often spoke in fragments, and he was used to it. If she wanted to talk to him, she would speak with a lower, whispery tone she selected when it was just the two of them.

"Almost there," Dean said, "I can feel it. The ancestral lands give me a weird feeling in my belly, and on my skin, like tiny invisible ants running across it. Too bad we have to take a helicopter there; I would just as soon change and run all the way!"

"Time is of the utmost importance," she replied. The two of them were supposed to have made it to the designated location, one of the mountain clan's villages deep in the Alaskan wilderness, last night. She knew it wasn't a huge matter of protocol, they would be there soon enough, but she still regretted how long it had taken to make the other preparations.

When she and Dean's father, Aaron, had called the

forum, thereby delaying the leadership and moving it to hallowed ground, she'd feared the old man's tactics. Most of the other packs and elders didn't care about internal elections, which is what she had been counting on. Now, they were going to be participating in it, and that meant a certain amount of charisma would determine the outcome.

She looked again at her brother. Dean was a stalwart and capable warrior, and she doubted if there were any – either in their own Pack or in other clans – that could best him in a physical contest. But there was more to leadership than simply being strong; one needed the mental faculty, the diplomatic sensitivity, to succeed. *That's where I come in,* she thought. The two of them were opposite sides of the same coin and together they were a formidable force.

But Nathan inhabited a balance between the two. Perhaps not as strong as Dean, or as cunning and intellectually operative as herself, but he represented both traits in a single person. That made him dangerous.

"Do you think the rogue group has already made it to the forum?" Dean asked, and she winced. Although he was dim, the fact they were twins seemed to alert him to some of her inner thoughts, especially when she didn't want him to be.

"They should be," she said.

For a moment, she thought of Nika, the human who had somehow found her way into the good graces of

Nathan and who had been living under the roof of their mansion back in Calgary. She was aware of the circumstances that caused this outsider to reside among them, whispers of an attack on her life, which she thought was dubious enough. *Who would dare attack a human in a public space,* she wondered.

Luckily, Nathan had been there to save her, but that didn't make Flores like her any more. She and Nathan had spent almost all their time together since the incident, and Flores had to admit she was jealous. Perhaps that was the nature of her dislike, but jealousy seemed a poor excuse for motive. Jealousy was a fickle emotion, and it would only compromise her logic. She shook her head.

She and Dean had gone behind the Pack's back, though.

After hearing about the forum, she had Dean contact some of the rogue groups of shifters who inhabited the northern lands. Flores didn't like the idea of taking the forum to Alaska, at least in Calgary she knew the terrain, but she could try and protect herself, Dean, and Nathan, she reflected. The rogue groups had responded, as she knew they would, to the incentive of money. *We'll have a mercenary force protecting the forum from the outside*, she thought. What the Pack did not know wouldn't hurt them.

The helicopter dove lower now, skimming over the tops of the trees. The pilot's voice issued through the headphones and both Dean and Flores became alert.

“There’s smoke up ahead,” he murmured.

“That’s not unusual,” Flores commented, more to herself than anyone, “the combined packs probably had a huge feast last night. They’re just bonfires.”

“I don’t think so,” the pilot insisted, and she and Dean looked out the window as the helicopter slowly descended.

What Flores saw made her tremble. The pilot was right. There was too much smoke, and it was scattered, coming from a dozen different places. Threads of black pushing skyward, losing itself in an aimless erosion of air as it went above the canopy of trees. Dean sensed his sister’s panic and gripped the armrest.

“Take us down, now,” Flores said.

“Those smoke pillars are still a way off… if that’s the village, it’s at least a couple kilometers—“

“Now!” Dean barked, echoing his sister’s command.

The pilot looked back at them through his aviators and hesitated a moment before reacting. If it was just Dean, or Flores, he might’ve had the resolve to keep flying, but together they were an impressive force. He reluctantly settled the helicopter toward a very small clearing between several pines. With the circumference of the rotors, the small craft barely fit, and even Flores felt her hand flexing on her knee as they came to a shuddering stop.

Dean already had the sliding door open and hopped down onto the grass mat underneath, his bald head pivoting left and right as he scanned the surrounding forest, still only partially illuminated by the infant sun. A fresh breeze inundated the compartment of the helicopter as Flores grabbed her leather satchel and flung it over her shoulder.

"What do you hope to accomplish?" the pilot barked over his shoulder, "It'll take you at least an hour through this bush to get to the village. I was only paid to take you there. If this is where you want—"

"It is," she said, "now go."

The pilot shook his head and Flores jumped out and ducked toward the tree line where Dean was waiting for her. Behind them, the craft purred and started to lift again. She watched its black shape nearly clear the tops of the trees.

"Flores, what—" Dean was about to ask, but was cut off by a sharp grating sound: metal crunching against metal, as if some behemoth monster were chewing on an automobile. Both twins turned toward the helicopter, which was listing perilously above them.

There was a black barb, feathered, sticking out of the chassis. Another whistling sound issued from the far side of the clearing and three more black streaks slammed through the plastic windshield of the helicopter. The sound cracked, ice-like, and two of the missiles pinned inward. The pilot didn't even have time to react as the heavy arrows stapled him to his feet. Flores saw him cough blood against the cockpit window, and then lean down on the controls. She barely had time to push Dean out of the way as the helicopter's rotors cut and split against tree trunks with a terrifying gnashing of steel and wood.

There was a small gap, infinitely quiet, as the two of them jumped down off the knoll toward a crisscrossing of fallen trees and logs in a small mossy gully below. Flores' breath caught in her throat. Then the explosion rocketed behind them, and a wave of heat blazed against her and Dean's backs and the ground loomed up. She grunted with the impact and made an effort to roll, but Dean was close behind her and simply wrapped his huge arms around her waist like a protective armor. The helicopter's chassis shattered and shrapnel flew over their heads. The smell of burning gasoline, and of nearby trees taking to the flame, covered them like ash.

"That was close," Dean groaned, opening his huge biceps and letting her loose. Blood pulsed crimson on half a dozen cuts and lacerations he'd acquired from the fall, and Flores felt ill with guilt that he had tried to protect her at the cost of his own safety. "You saw the arrows, Flores? Someone's still here."

"I know," she hissed, angrier with herself for not having anticipated the unpredictable, "Those arrows were too powerful to be from humans. And I smell shifters."

"Me too," he whimpered. "What do we do, Flores?"

She thought about it. The attack on the helicopter had confirmed her suspicions, that the multiple smoke signs she'd seen from the village hadn't been mere bonfires. *The forum was attacked*, she thought. But how, and by whom? This was precisely what she'd hoped to avoid when hiring the mercenary rogue wolves.

"We have to get to the village, see what happened there," she said, peering over the gully. There was no sign of anyone, human or shifter. But if they were dealing with northern wolves, those who had grown up in the wilderness and knew it by heart, then even the shadows between the trees might be an enemy. "The pilot wasn't wrong, it'll take us forty minutes at the very least to get to the village, and that's if we're moving fast and straight. I don't like it, though."

"We're being hunted," Dean said, and crouched low, his huge hands covering the stony perch they'd landed on like some flesh colored glove.

"Yes, we are," she said. "We need to flush them out, first. Take off your shirt, Dean."

"Why?" he asked, even though he was already obeying.

"I'm going to set a trap, and let them spring it," she smirked, her short pixie hair bristling. Her lean figure slid backward down the lip of the gully again, every moment slick and fluid as a fox.

Dean simply shook his head, his simian brows arched

in a confused perturbation. “I don’t understand,” he admitted.

“They’re hunting us,” she said, “So I’ll let them. But when they find their prey, I’m the only one they’ll see. You, dear brother, will have to be fast. We’ll get one chance. Can you do it?”

“I’d never let anything happen to you,” he said stubbornly.

Flores smiled, a rare smile that wasn’t born of cunning or deception, but rather a tacit recognition that as dim as her twin brother might’ve been, he had certain qualities even Nathan couldn’t live up to.

“I know,” she said, drawing her thin fingers across his sallow cheek.

CHAPTER NINE

The morning passed into day and began to grow hot, and by that time, Nika and Nathan struggled out of their makeshift cave with the warmth on their skin. Both were naked, and their skin glistened with the salty residue of sweat.

Nika's round face looked outward, back toward the village where they'd escaped. Her small nose flared as she inhaled, and she squeezed her fingers between Nathan's. Both looked like a primeval icon, the first Adam and Eve, looking out across an untapped Eden. But it was far from paradise. Nika felt a lump grow in her throat. Memories were something neither of the lovers could escape; the smell of death, the screams of the villagers falling prey to black shafted arrows. The cold unflinching cruelty of the wooden masked riders, and the haunting eyes of their bloodlust.

At least Clara and the children are safe, she thought, recalling Nathan's steadfast sister. She had a heartbroken look on her face when she'd hugged her brother goodbye and turned without a second look. Both siblings were bound by different duties: Clara's was to protect the young ones from the raiders while Nathan's was to protect Clara.

"How are you feeling?" Nika asked, letting go of his hand and turning toward him.

Her perfectly round breasts bounced against her chest, finding their own shadows hidden underneath their weight. Her pink nipples glowed with the sunshine, and the graceful arc of her buttocks flexed as she shifted her weight to the other leg.

Nathan's long black hair clouded his face, and he craned to look at the small puncture wounds in his shoulder and the scratches on his rib cage. They had all closed, and there was no blood. But even his shifter regenerative abilities would need more than a few hours to heal the deeper wounds.

"Fine," he insisted, "Stiff, but fine."

Nika bit her lip, and another gust of wind blew at her dark hair, tickling it against the curve of her spine. Nathan reached out and stroked the top of her back and she stiffened for a moment and then relaxed.

"No stopping you," she thought. "Can you walk?"

He nodded, and rubbed his chin where a day's worth of whisker was coming in like an overcast insinuation. It strengthened the outline of his face, and his heavy dark eyebrows pressed down on his rectangular gaze. Nika saw everything there she expected -- kindness, love, fear.

"I'll change again," he said, stepping back, "if we're going to get back to the village, it'll be fast for you to ride on me. In my wolf form, I have a better chance of healing faster, too."

She nodded and stepped back, picked up the scattered clothes she had laid against bare south-facing granite stone to dry them. She pulled on her panties and mud-streaked jeans. Her bra had snapped during her fight with the raiders earlier in the morning, and she sniffed and tossed it to one side, pulling on the borrowed button up shirt. Her breasts pushed out against it provocatively, and though a few buttons had been sheared off, it was tight enough to bundle her bosom comfortably.

Meanwhile, Nathan bent over on his knees and ducked his head. Nika had seen his transformation once before, it was still unnerving and uncomfortable to see him change from a human into a wolf. The sound of tendons stretching, muscles ripping and resealing, bones snapping and lengthening, was almost enough to make her sick to her stomach. She could only imagine how painful it was for him each time, but he never protested or made any complaints.

In moments, his hind legs had extended outward, their nails carving deep grooves into the hard packed earth and a swift brushy tail pushed out behind and swiped at the air. Unlike the other wolves and shifters she'd seen, Nathan's wolf-form was unique, with its dark gray pattern forming around his back.

He made a growling sound and licked at the pink wounds on his side that peeked out behind his fur. He made a few trundling steps toward Nika. She bent down and rubbed his head again, feeling his noble yellow eyes fasten to her. He nuzzled at her, and she threw one leg over him. His muscles rippled under her thighs as she tightened her grip and wrapped her fists into the fur of his collar. The warm musty scent of his pelt drifted over her, and she breathed it in deep, trying to place it in her memory for all time.

Slowly, Nathan backtracked the way they came, while she rode upright. When they reached the narrow ridge where they'd met the three raiders, she had to look away from the tangled bodies below. One of the shifters had returned to his normal human form, and his naked corpse was half-submerged in the creek. She put a hand to her mouth and Nathan began their descent down the backside of the ridge.

By time they made it to the junction that led back to the village, Nika's pulse was racing again. A steady hammer of blood pounded between her ears. Soon, the smell of smoke assaulted them both, and Nathan's pace broke into a lope as they breached through the thicket into the clearing. Nika hopped off, her arms limp as she surveyed the devastation.

A number of the longhouses had been burnt to the ground, and those that stood, bore the evidence of flame and battle. Smoke clotted the air, creating a veil of acrid blue. Nathan growled and his paws pressed squarely into the mud as he advanced, his black lips raised over dagger-sized fangs. With the dire wolf, Nika felt a bit safer, but even so, she reached out toward him, keeping one hand firmly knotted in his fur.

There were moans and screams, cries of pain and anguish alike. Here and there, corpses, both of villagers and raiders peppered the land. Nika retched and covered her nose again – in the heat of the midday sun, flies had already found their way to the dead, and wrapped in cowls of mud.

"My god," she implored.

Up ahead, there were several groups clustered around some of the less-razed buildings. Standing among them, going from villager to villager, Nika recognized Corin, the chief. When he saw the two of them moving through the swathe of smoke like ghosts, his stony complexion revealed the pain he felt. Nika stared at what remained of his people; men and women were huddled on makeshift beds and stretchers, many of them contorted in pain. She saw deep wounds and gashes on almost all of them. Hardly anyone had come away from the raider's attack unscathed. She knelt down and helped one of the young women, her head bandaged with dirty rags, to sip from a water flask.

"Corin…" she murmured, but there were no words to convey the extent of what she felt.

"I knew the two of you would succeed," he said, "The children? Tell me the children are safe."

"They are," Nika said, "Clara's with them. We lured the raiders away. But what happened here? Is this… is this all of us?"

Corin sighed and sat down with a huff on a tree stump, his wooden mallet perched on one thigh. His dark sandstone skin was flecked with mud and charcoal, and he could only shake his head at the chaos around them. Nathan reverted to a human shape and scowled.

"We did our best to hold them off," Corin said, and tossed a dirty pair of doeskin breeches at Nathan who unashamedly pulled them on. His naked torso was ripped with a barely containable anger, and Nika wondered if he would ever be able to untighten his fists. "But they were too many, and we too few. So many of us dead…"

Nika felt her eyes tear up. "We need to get help," she begged.

The chief nodded. "Aye, some of us – the hunters who were not injured – were sent out to the other villages. All we can do now is wait. And hope."

"I should've stayed," Nathan replied, kneeling over the body of an old man in the mud. With so few able-bodied villagers left, and those without grievous injuries tending to those who couldn't stand, there hadn't been time to gather the dead. "I should have done something."

"You did what any good Alpha would do," Corin replied grimly.

"He's right, Nathan," Nika replied. The woman in her arms nodded thankfully and leaned back down on the stretcher.

"What happened, Corin?" he demanded, "We can't stay here. If the raiders return, we won't be a match for them."

The old chief stood up again, limping on one leg where a huge purple bruise had swollen against the side of one kneecap. "The raiders are gone," he said fixedly, "after you and Nika left, I was sure that we would be slaughtered, there was no doubt in my mind. As long as the young ones escaped, I could live with dying, as long as I died taking a few of the bastards with me. Then, things began to turn, we gained a foothold and were able to hold off their arrows.

I tried to send our numbers in opposite directions to confuse the enemy, hoping that at least some of us might get through, but it was useless. They were too fast, and had fully encircled the camp. That's when they lit their arrows. Flames started up everywhere, and the small protective cluster we had formed began to dissolve in panic.

But then, suddenly, the arrows stopped. There were screams from the forest but it was not us. The screams were coming from the raiders. We huddled in fear, waiting for our deaths but they never came," Corin continued, "and then as if by magic, everything was very still again. Through the smoke I saw a man approaching, and I recognized his insignia as belonging to one of the rogue groups of wolves that live in the vast barrens."

"The rogue groups were responsible for the attack?" Nathan ventured.

"No," Corin said, as if he still couldn't believe it, "In fact, they'd been ordered and paid to protect the forum. But they'd arrived moments too late. When they got here, they found us already under attack. They made quick kills of the raiders, and were able to run off the few remaining stragglers. We've been waiting for them to return."

Nika shook her head. "Wait, what do you mean?"

Nathan was equally interested and took a step forward. "Someone paid rogue wolves to *protect* the forum… not to attack it?" he reached down and snatched Corin's mallet away and let it hang like a blood-soaked augury in his hand. It didn't make any sense. The forum had been called and held here, on ancestral lands, in order to make the procession of leadership more secure. Only the Pack – only the elders – had known about it, and its sudden announcement would have made it impossible for anyone to plan and mount this sort of attack. "Who paid them?"

Corin shrugged again. "You'll have to ask them when they get back," Corin said, "but I think we can assume there's more going on here than meets the eye. If the raiders were part of a conspiracy that started within the Pack, it would explain how easily they managed to subdue us."

"But now, there's evidence someone was trying to protect the forum all along by hiring rogues," Nathan nodded, and threw the mallet into the earth at his feet where it stuck in and wobbled.

"What about Aaron?" Nika asked, "I don't see him here."

The name of Nathan's uncle made both men freeze and they drooped their heads. Nika realized reality was something you couldn't fight against, no matter how hard you tried. Eventually, it always won, and you were left to pick up the pieces, gluing them together. But she was beyond running any longer, her tears carved channels through the dusty ash on both cheeks.

"Haven't seen 'im," Corin admitted, "and I looked. He's not among the dead, here."

"So he's still alive?" she said, letting herself indulge in hope.

Corin opened his mouth to say something but his beady eyes were distracted by something in the distance near the tree line, another shape quivering in the silhouette of smoke. It was a man, and his arms were the size of tree trunks, and he looked as if he was drawn by an artist who exaggerated every feature. He was naked, and as he came closer to the three of them, they could only gape. Cradled in the massive nest of his arms was an unconscious woman. Nika mouthed her name.

Flores.

CHAPTER TEN

"We were attacked," Dean reported, standing up. He'd tied a small sheet around his waist as a loincloth, looking like a contemporary Tarzan, except for the bald dome of his lumpy head. He looked back down at his sister. Flores was shivering and pale, there was a bloody puncture in her abdomen. Nika and Corin stooped and tended to her, washing away the blood.

"It's deep, and she's lost a lot of blood," Corin said glumly.

"Please save her," Dean pleaded. He looked like a stone golem that suddenly suffered the loss of its master and was on the verge of disappearing into dust himself. "We tried to get to the village as soon as possible. But… but I wasn't strong enough. I couldn't fight them all off, they just kept coming."

He looked at his hands, which were ruddy with dried blood, none of it his own.

Nathan swallowed and stood beside his cousin. "The raiders," he said, "They must have seen the helicopters and followed it. Probably didn't want any witnesses." He didn't ask whether or not he and Flores had been behind the attack – it was clear from Dean's simple and predictable nature that the twins had been targeted just like the rest of them.

I feel like an idiot, he thought suddenly. For days, he had suspected Flores of being behind the first attack on Nika. After Aaron told them all about his and Clara's bloodline, the unique transgenic gene that could turn other humans into shifters, he had suspected as much from the cruel and cunning woman who so efficiently alienated herself from the rest of the Pack.

He patted Dean on the shoulder and crouched down beside Nika as he touched Flores' forehead. Her skin was pale and cool to the touch, and he understood the symptoms as well as Corin, who refused to look up from his work. He re-applied a small bandage of scavenged material and some of the antiseptic herbs he'd managed to find among the ruins of one of the longhouses.

Flores opened her eyes suddenly as he knelt over her, and there was wild-eyed fear glazed across them like a sickening veneer. But there was also lucidity, and she shivered again, and coughed. "Hello, cousin," she murmured.

"Rest easy, Flores," he said, "You're hurt pretty bad."

"I know it," she said, and managed a smile as another series of convulsions overtook her. Nika helped to hold her down. The skinny pixie took in a deep breath. "Thought I could lure them out. There was an army of them. Dean was amazing, he really was. He killed them all with his bare hands. But it wasn't… enough. Don't let him blame himself, yeah?" she said.

Behind them, Dean started to whimper and big

pathetic tears coursed down his cheeks and landed on the bare bridge of his chest. Nathan gripped Flores' hand and stroked her forehead again. "He's pretty magnificent, hey?" he nodded.

"Just like you," Flores said, "I never told you… that I had a crush on you, did I? Seems silly to say it out loud, now doesn't it? I… I never wanted you to become Alpha, Nathan. I knew that you didn't even see me – not like I saw you. I thought, if Dean became Alpha then maybe… maybe…"

"It's alright," Nathan said, and looked up at Corin who shook his head in the most subtle way he knew how, "That doesn't matter right now, okay? I see you. I see you."

She smiled again, and Nika's heart curled up into its shell like a snail. For so long she hated the short-haired devilish woman, had feared her, but she couldn't anymore. Her blood-drained face was serene in a way she had never seen before, and the smile was honest, complicit with its own understanding of its transience. Nika covered her mouth again and let out a sob.

Flores looked up and grinned at the human, and raised her skinny hand toward her. Nika took it, surprised at how soft and warm it was. "Wasn't fair to you," she said, "I think… I envied you. Take care of him, okay? He's… he's so stubborn and stupid and blind sometimes, especially to things right in front of him. Do that, okay?" Nika nodded frantically. "Good," Flores let her hand go and blinked upward at the blue expanse of sky, “We could have been sisters. I would have… liked that.”

“Flores, stay with us!” Nathan pleaded.

“I tried to protect us, all of us,” she said, her eyes closing, “I tried to protect you.”

“You did!” he said, shaking her arms, but she was already gone.

Dean took two steps back and fell onto his knees and buried his head against the ground, pulling at the thick folds of his neck and head with both meaty palms as he wept and howled pitiably. Corin stood up and gently placed his hands over his eyes, and looked to Nathan for guidance. Instead, Nathan stood back up and gazed down at his cousin for half an instant before he tipped his head back and howled. His lips formed an O and he joined in Dean’s howl. It was an eerie piercing scream, something rooted in a millennia that Nika could only admire from afar.

Corn tilted his head as well and joined in, and one after another, each villager did the same. For some, it was painful to sit up or to expel breath, but there was an urgency in their collective call, a mythological wariness of their own descent. It was a howl for the dead, a way to signal their souls back to the woods where they belonged. But it was also meant for the living, for those who had survived and would carry on the legacy and memory of the fallen. It became a polysyllabic lull, an unearthly music that joined the smoke of the fallen village, ushering in a shared memory of hunts.

Nika felt tears growing in her eyes again, and couldn't stop them from streaming down her face, blinding her. Absently, without thinking, she raised her own lips and let out a bleating cry that joined the chorus. No one stopped her or admonished her, she had shed blood just the same as them, and even if she was a human at heart and in blood, she had earned her place here amongst them. She had earned her own howl. But this one she sang for Flores.

The mystery of the rogue wolves had been her doing. All along, Flores had only been trying to strengthen the security of the forum. *If she hadn't enlisted their help, then the village would have been completely destroyed*, Nika realized. She felt a sudden and immediate pity for the woman, whose only real crime had been a sinister devotion to the two most important men in her life: Dean and Nathan. In the end, it killed her. *But not before she saved scores of us*, Nika said. That's how she would remember Flores.

At long last, the cry died out, and a great stillness pervaded through the clearing. Corin returned to the villagers and Nika helped him administer whatever herbs he had left and to bind the wounds of those injured. Nathan helped, but they all worked with a wordless sense of desperation. By evening, they had built crude lean-tos for the sick and those who would not survive the night. Both Nathan and Nika pushed themselves into occupying every spare moment with creating more shelters or ferrying water from the creek or trying to console those in pain. When they confronted each other, they only permitted themselves a single look, always the same. There were too many words, and at the same time not enough, and so they could only reconcile the company of another with a glance, as if to say *it's enough.*

By sundown, several strangers appeared on the tree line. Corin gestured at Nathan. The chief looked weary, his eyes sagged and empty of anything but fatigue, and Nathan nodded and strode out to meet them. Nika followed behind, but stopped when he shot her a look, this one equating to *hold back.*

The captain of the rogue wolves was a young man about Nathan's age. He had thick brown dreadlocks tightly bundled into a braid that wound its way down his back. Like the others, he bore a number of scars on his bare chest, and his pants were roughly sewn together with rawhide, and looked like untanned leather. A heavy reek of humus and sweat seethed off his muscular frame. His two brothers crouched low at his side, one in human form the other still a wolf with a grey and silver complexion.

"Who might you be?" the captain said, and planted a six-foot long spear fire-hardened at one end, into the dirt at his feet. "Where's Corin?"

"Here, Alex," Corin said, "but this is Nathan. The newest Alpha."

Nathan shook his head. "That hasn't been decided

yet," he held up his hand.

A monotonous voice from behind broke the spell, and they all turned to see Dean rising from a fallen log. The sheet loincloth around his waist was soiled with grime and with blood from helping the others tend to the wounded. For several hours, he had loomed over the body of his sister, keeping vigil. A veil of cedar boughs had been draped across her, in part to conceal her body, and also to keep the flies and other pests at bay.

"It has been decided," Dean said, his eyes narrowing like flint shards, "it would have been what Flores wanted – what she *really* wanted, I mean. I withdraw my birthright and give you my support, Nathan. But on one condition." Nathan stared at his cousin, seeing a side of him come to light that none of them had known existed.

"What is it?"

"You will find who killed Flores. And when you do, you will let *me* kill them."

Nathan swallowed hard, considering, even though he knew he had already accepted it. Dean and Flores had been inseparable, almost as inseparable as he and Clara, but the twins had shared a different kind of bond, one he had no real hope of understanding fully. He simply nodded and turned back to Alex. The captain slapped his wrists.

"Flores is dead," he confirmed and looked toward the

bundle of cedar boughs, "She was the one who hired us. Figures we got here too late but if she's dead, then I guess you're the one we report to?" Nathan remained sullen, and Alex shrugged. "We got good news and bad news. Bad news is, me brothers got a little carried away and dismembered near every last one of the buggers. Strange shifters, too… all of them wearing things like this."

Alex tossed a wooden mask at Nathan. One side of it was broken off, and a sticky black substance had dried on one jagged edge. He held it up, his own blue eye piercing through the remaining eyepiece. He dropped it in the mud and crunched his heel into it.

"What's the good news?" he asked unceremoniously.

The captain seemed to appreciate Nathan's cold enthusiasm and winked, snapping his fingers. His clan brother, the one in human form and similarly dressed with only deer-hide pants and what looked like moccasins, gave a blunt nod and ran back into the tree line.

"Good news is, at least *one* of my horde managed to keep his jaws away from the jugular, so to speak. We got one of the raiders who tried to leave, but truth be told, he was mauled pretty badly. Doubt he'll live much longer but if you want to get something out of him—"

"Bring him," Nathan said, and turned back as he walked towards the remains of Corin's longhouse. The rafters had broken in on one side where flame had eaten through, but there were still three walls that faced away from the makeshift camp.

Nika watched him, and looked to Corin, but the old wolf was looking in the same direction. Something in Nathan had changed since the battle. No, more precisely, since Flores had died. She saw it in the way he carried himself, as if he were moving on autopilot, letting his body react to some automatic stimulus. The part of him she had fallen in love with, the part that was kind, that could smile even at the worst of times, that would make inappropriate jokes if only to alleviate the tension of the darkest hour – was inert. In its place, there was a new and transformed Nathan. One who had taken up the mantle of the Alpha like his parents before him, not out of obligatory duty, not out of greed or desire, but from necessity.

"A man who chooses power is never capable of wielding it," Corin remarked after Nathan had walked past, and Nika realized it was meant for her.

From the tree line, two more human shifters emerged, both men naked from the waist up, these unaligned rogues of the north. Between them was a skinnier man, covered in dried blood and barely able to stand. One eye was swollen shut, and a thin whisper of drool eked out of his broken lips. Nika gulped and watched helplessly. He may have been an enemy but she couldn't help but think, *this isn't right*.

"Corin, what are they going to do to him?" she asked, not sure she wanted to know the answer.

The chief didn't reply, and clucked his tongue. One of the villagers was asking for water. He ducked his head and disappeared under the lean-to, leaving Nika to ponder the rhetorical nature of her question. She saw a certain fazed anger in the faces of the other shifters; all of their heads were craned toward the longhouse.

She shook her head. *They're going to kill him*, she thought. No, it was worse than that, the battered raider had been near death as it was, but they were going to interrogate him until he finally perished. A sick feeling rocked her world, and she had to reach out to steady herself against one of the braces of the shelter. *How could things have gotten so bad,* she thought.

For a moment, she wished for her other life. The one where she only had to worry about what to wear the next day, or what sort of new alcoholic beverage her roommate James had cooked up in her absence. The life where she was a director of an art gallery, and life had its simple predictable mechanisms, a routine that would always be there for her no matter what. Nika balked when she realized she *couldn't* wish for that life anymore. For better or worse, she had left it in the past, and embraced a new one, one she didn't know the end of, nor where it would lead.

She picked herself up and walked briskly toward the longhouse, steeling herself. The raider might've been responsible for killing the villagers in cold blood, and she couldn't fault them for their feelings, but neither could she ignore her own feelings. As she neared the longhouse, one of the raiders appeared and stood in front of her. A muted scream drawled from behind the wall, and her face tightened.

"Let me through," she hissed, "I have to see Nathan."

He merely shook his head, and another scream came out of nowhere and she gasped, only to suddenly be cut off abruptly. Nika took a step back, her eyes wide with terror, and she covered her mouth. An instant later, Nathan walked out, his face was harder than she'd ever seen, as if he'd carved it himself out of granite and then let it harden under a glacial stream. When he saw her, his eyes widened for a moment, whether in fear or surprise, Nika couldn't tell, but he dropped his head again and started to walk past her.

What compelled her to reach out and grab his arm, she didn't know. The previous day's events hadn't hit her yet, not like they would in the weeks to come. She could understand that objectively, that she was still in shock, and was glad for it. But there was another feeling she couldn't delay, and it wrapped around her chest like fishing line and pulled tight. She'd seen Nathan kill before – in the ambush he had speared one of the shifters through the chest – and while it was traumatic, and the scarred face of her attacker still lingered in her mind if she let it wander, that at least had been in self-defense, in the heat of the moment.

Her eyes clouded with tears again as she gazed at the half-burnt wall of the longhouse. The lowly scream of agony cut short rung like a bell in her ears, and her hand tightened on his arm. He didn't look in her direction, but stopped, his head downcast at the mud.

"Nathan," she murmured.

"We need to go," he enunciated, "Alex has sent his scouts ahead. They'll be here by morning to help take the wounded. Let's get them prepared."

"Nathan," she pleaded again, and her hand dropped from his wrist.

She wanted him to say something, to defend his actions -- anything, but he remained silent. After a breath, he continued walking past her. His footsteps were as soft as the death of an animal dying alone. Nika couldn't look at the longhouse any longer, and she wept again as she stood, unable to go forward to look at what Nathan had accomplished in his anger and his need for revenge.

CHAPTER ELEVEN

Time did its little trick of passing quicker than Nika could apprehend. It all became a jumbled arrangement of moments, a blur of helicopters landing and affiliated packs carrying out the wounded from the burned village. Corin was the last to leave on the final helicopter, along with her and Nathan. He stood an interminably long time as they waited under the umbrella drone of the rotors. All around him were the last vestiges of daylight, and still the sour smell of smoke. When he finally turned away from the wreckage and joined them, he was silent. Nika didn't remember him speaking the rest of the way back to Anchorage.

Nika was relieved to see that Clara and the children had already made it there, having followed the creek downstream until they found a logging road and were picked up by a very befuddled logger. Nathan's stolid grimness dissipated for a moment when he saw her, and they embraced. But as soon as they pulled away again, the same aloofness had settled like silt across his face. When Clara tried to ask Nika about it in private, she didn't know what to say, and could only shake her head.

At the human settlement, they said goodbye to Corin and his people. Alex, the captain of the rogue wolves, once again offered his services to Nathan, this time without any expectations of payment. They may have been wild men of the north, without any true leadership or alliances, but that didn't mean they had forgotten their shifter ways. The very idea that another wolf pack could so easily kill men and women without a single regard had sickened the rogues.

"I'm not going with you," Dean said at last, meeting them at the Anchorage airport where another helicopter would take them back to the hidden landing field where their jet was waiting. Clara stepped forward, took his right hand between hers and kissed it.

"Where will you go?" she asked her cousin.

Dean scratched his head and looked back at Corin. "I want to help these villagers, as best as I can. I think, if Flores were alive, she'd want me to do that. She wasn't really cruel, you know. Maybe she didn't think I could keep up with her, but I knew her. She was my twin, after all. She would have wanted me to stay here and help them rebuild." His big cow-like eyes lifted toward the sky. "Besides, I want to intern her body here, on the ancestral lands, so that her spirit will find its way back to the others. I think... there is another Pack waiting for her, up there. I want to make sure she gets there safely."

Clara bit back her tears and they landed on Dean's hand. "She would have liked that, Dean," she admitted. "You're always welcome back to our Den. You know that."

"I know, Clara," he said, and his ogre smile drew

upwards. "Nathan, you made me a promise," he restated to the new Alpha, who stood off to one side, his hands dipped into the pockets of a second-hand fleece, "I'll be waiting."

As the helicopter lifted, Dean waved at them once and stood watching, and Nika watched him turn into a small dot and then disappear entirely. Her stomach opened up again with a feeling of loss. She wondered what would happen to the poor brute. Clara and Nathan had always painted him as a lost sort of child, someone who needed his hand held, but she saw now they had all been mistaken. Even Flores. *He's going to be alright,* she thought. Eventually, they would all be.

The helicopter let them off at the field and all three waited patiently for it to depart. The owner, a bush pilot and a human local from Anchorage, had been paid to take them to this location and drop them off, no questions asked. After Clara had shown him a sheaf of bills, he had agreed without a second thought, but they saw him shaking his head through the windshield as he lifted and steered his nose back to the coast. After he'd gone, Nathan quickly trudged to where camouflage tarps had been thrown over the plane and stepped inside ahead of them, lost in his own world, and Clara finally grabbed Nika by the arm and stopped her.

"Nika, there's something you're not telling me," she whispered, and then let go of her, "and I think you probably think you have good reason to. But if it's something to do with my brother, if not telling me is putting him in more danger… I won't forgive you for that."

Nika bristled with anger, even though it was misplaced. She was angry with Nathan, but also with herself for allowing him to slide so quickly into his own private darkness. The muffled scream of the surviving raider still haunted her, and sometimes she would turn and look around, thinking his ghost might actually be there behind her, bloody and one-eyed. *Charging me with guilt*, she thought.

"I…" Nika felt the words mingle together like watercolors, all of it a haphazard mess, incoherent, and shook her head again. "I can't right now, Clara. I don't know if it's even my right anymore. Ask Nathan yourself when we get back to Calgary."

"You think he'll actually talk to me?" she said, and Nika saw now how worried Clara had actually been. Less than a day ago, she had to say goodbye to her brother, not knowing whether she would ever see him again. While they had reunited, it was like she truly *had* lost him. The brother she returned to wasn't the same one she left behind, and her own hue of guilt was stricken across her features.

"I don't know," Nika admitted.

"I tried to talk to him back in Anchorage. I asked about Aaron, and he just turned away from me, like you just did. Did he die, Nika?"

Nika shook her head. "I don't know."

"What do you mean you *don't know*?" Clara snapped, tightening her hand on Nika's arm until it stung, even through the thick borrowed jumper she had on, and when she saw the human's face contort in pain, she instantly let go. "I… I'm sorry, Nika. I didn't mean—"

"We couldn't find his body," she replied, "I looked. I looked all over. But…"

Clara sighed and rushed forward, hugging the younger woman and Nika was surprised by the sudden act of compassion. She was surprised more by the free flow of tears that streamed down her own face, and the sudden missive of sobs that ached out of her as she buried her face into Clara's chest and felt strong wiry arms fold like around her like a filial cape.

"It's okay," Clara whispered, "okay, now."

Nika pulled away and wiped her cheeks. The anxiety that had coiled itself inside her had partially been sprung by Clara's hug, but the dull ache against her chest where her heart was could not be alleviated. "Nathan… I can't right now," Nika said.

"I'll talk to him," Clara promised, "Let's get on board. Get some sleep."

"I think Nathan trusts you," Nika said, "more than me."

It was a terrible admission, but she knew it was true

on some level. Who was she to him anyway? A human date that had ended badly. Neither of them had chosen this, and while they tried to make the best of it, it didn't erase the fact that they were ultimately acquaintances. *Are we though*, she wondered, remembering again the times they had loved, the tenderness they shared in the cave. Was it all just a symptom of shock? Something cracked inside her like glass as she considered the possibility, and she wasn't sure it would ever heal over. Tears formed in the corners of her eyes and she turned away from Clara.

"That's not true," Clara said under her breath, but Nika had already made it to the gangway and was halfway up the stairs. The cold Alaskan wind drove down from the north, and the older woman gave a final glance at the ancestral land. Like Nathan, it too had changed, but too subtly to localize; like a differential, a pressure variance. *A shadow sliding over one eye*, she thought.

On board, Nika curled up, hugging her knees, and tried to sleep. Nathan was on the other side of the aisle, one fist under his chin as he gazed ponderously out of the window and the diminishing landscape under them. She was torn between wanting to talk to him, and realizing they had nothing to talk about, at least, nothing she could reasonably approach him with, without breaking down. The sensation of not even being able to talk to him was unbearable, and she shut her eyes tighter, trying not to sob.

She didn't see him raise his head off his chin to look at her before she passed out. If she had, she might've felt reassurance at the reflection of that first spark that she had fallen in love with -- the kindness of a wolf that had, at long last, and after too much loss, found a mate.

*

It was quiet in the mansion for two days. Nika let James know she was okay, and would be returning soon but that she had some "unfinished business" to take care of. When she wouldn't be any more specific, the flamboyant man huffed loudly into the speaker and agreed not to call the police. *At least he hasn't lost his sense of humor,* Nika thought, hanging up. Evening was coming on fast again, and the tea Clara had brewed for her was cold and lifeless. She sipped at it, made a distasteful look, and set it back down again.

Clara had left again, though she wouldn't tell them where – something to do with checking up on some of her sources, Nika didn't know what she hoped to discover. There were so many unanswered questions. The raiders hadn't been Flores' idea, so that meant *another* enemy was waiting in the shadows, one that was even more well connected than they thought.

She phoned the gallery next and told them she needed another few days off. Her manager, once again, seemed overjoyed about the idea. She still had nearly a month of paid vacation time that had accrued over the years. Her phone clicked off and she set it next to the cup and crossed her legs. Calgary's city lights were coming on slowly.

She knew that eventually she would have to confront Nathan about what had happened, but it was like a thunderstorm on the horizon. You could try to run from it, but the weather always moved faster, and never tired. The proverbial tortoise in a terrestrial race, the top room in the west spire was alight, though she couldn't see anyone in Nathan's room. It took her another five minutes to will up the courage. She sipped down the rest of the tea and slapped her knees. *No point in waiting*, she thought. She needed to talk to him – neither of them had shared any more than a phrase here and there, and he had been anything but close since the two of them returned to the village to find it burned.

At the top of the circular staircase, she paused for a moment, and felt her heart thump again as she raised her knuckle and gave two short raps. For a moment, there wasn't a sound, and she wondered if he had heard.

"Come in," a gravelly voice growled from inside.

She gulped and turned the door handle slowly and stepped inside. Nika realized she'd never been in Nathan's room before, and was surprised by the simplicity of it. Unlike the other rooms and corridors of the mansion, which oozed of opulence and Victorian sensibilities long outdated, Nathan's room was the antithesis. It was also much smaller than the other bedrooms, and awkwardly shaped in a sort of oblong hexagram. Through a double skylight, the stars blinked on one by one, peering through the blue atmosphere.

Nathan was crouched over a small writing desk and had on simple pajama bottoms and an open bath robe with the sash untied. His abdominal muscles crimped as he huddled over the desk. He looked up from his writing, half-surprised to see Nika staring at him from the doorway, holding one of her elbows with her other hand.

"Nika," he murmured.

"I-I'm sorry, I didn't know you were busy," she said and lifted one heel off the floor to turn.

"No," he set the pen down and stood up awkwardly, his hands at his sides, "No, it's alright, really. Nothing that can't wait – and you wouldn't have come up here if it wasn't important. What's going on?"

She was taken aback for a moment by his cheerful and light-hearted attitude. How could he have simply overlooked and forgotten the way he'd treated her earlier? His face betrayed no evidence he had ever been anything other than his usual genial self. It disheartened her and revived her anger again as she closed the door behind her loudly enough to make him jump.

"You tell me," she murmured, "how about the fact you've turned into a murderer?"

The word *murderer* hung in the air like a non sequitur, and Nathan's brow furrowed as he picked up his pen and tapped it absently against the paper before dropping it again. "Come here," he urged, inviting her toward a couch that was against one wall and hedged by a bookshelf crowded with some works she recognized and plenty she didn't.

"I would rather stay here," she said, rubbing her elbow again.

For the first time, he saw how much he had alienated her, and winced at the circumspection and agony he had unwittingly caused in his lover. "We all did things back there, things we weren't proud of," he said cautiously.

"I didn't," she shook her head, "Except once. Trusting you to do the right thing."

The accusation hit home, and he sat down on the couch and planted his hands between his head. "You're talking about the survivor, aren't you? The one that Alex brought to me." He waited for a brief glint of comprehension to ignite behind Nika's glower, and then nodded. "I had to make it seem as if I'd killed him. He was the last of the raiders, and the villagers were watching. We may have inducted ourselves into human society but we are still wolves at heart. Law demanded justice."

"Justice doesn't mean killing an unarmed man at your mercy! He was barely able to stand on his own two feet!" Nika screamed at him, her face going purple with rage. All the things she'd been holding in came out in a single outburst, and he again flinched back as if he'd drawn too close to a flame. "If that's justice, I want no part of it."

"I didn't kill him," Nathan responded, and waited again for Nika to digest it.

"I saw. I heard him—"

"I said I needed to make it seem as if I'd killed him. Not only for the villagers' benefits and Corin's, but for my own," he explained. "You were there. Corin and Dean both admitted me as the Alpha, in front of everyone. Like it or not, I am the Alpha now – and all eyes were on me for my first command, my first decision. It had be a show of strength. But I didn't kill him."

"Then what—" Nika blurted again, taking steps forward, her bare feet staggering toward him.

"Alex and I asked him questions. And when I'd learned what I needed to know," Nathan hesitated again and was caught on the edge of divulging something, unsure of whether or not he should – a lesson, perhaps, he had learned from Flores; when to hold your cards, and when to show them. "You remember when we went into the shack out back, you, me, Clara and Aaron?"

"Of course, I remember," she said, remembering. At that time, she had been too shaken, too afraid of circumstances, to have much of an appetite. "I remember. But what does that have to do with the raider? What happened to him?"

Nathan stood back up, and his bathrobe parted down the middle. Nika wanted to touch his chest, the supple rise of each pectoral muscle. To feel the warmth of his body pressed against her again. But she couldn't escape a lingering revulsion.

"I let him go," Nathan said. "Rather, I had one of Alex's men shepherd him into the forest and tend to his wounds. He was more useful to me alive. Despite what you may think of me – what Clara, and Corin, and the others now think of me – I'm not heartless. I had to make it seem as if I were. It was imperative."

"Why?" she shook her head.

He sighed again and stepped forward to hug her. "In time," he said, "when Clara comes back, we will have another meeting, I'll tell you what I know. Both of you. Until then, I can't afford to be wrong and give false hope."

Nika screwed up her lips. His explanation, and the fact he now seemed back to normal, was encouraging, but she didn't like being kept in the dark. "You didn't have to be cold to me," she said, and he motioned her closer. This time she moved toward him and sat down on his knee. He put an arm around her and kissed her bare arm.

"I'm sorry for that, Nika, truly…" he grimaced, "but again, there's been so much to sift through. I shouldn't have ignored you."

"No, you shouldn't," she pouted, not letting him off

that easily. He finally smiled and moved his hand across her belly. She closed her eyes, and put her hand on top of his. "Then apologize."

Nathan reached up, guided her cheek toward his face, and kissed her. She kissed him back, clutching at the sides of his head as her lips plastered against his, moving in gentle movements until he reached around her and rolled her onto her back on the couch. Her limpid eyes blushed into his, looking for the man she loved. He was there, as perhaps he always had been, even under the veil of secrets and deceptions. *Nathan.*

He kissed her again, pushing his tongue between her lips until she sighed and opened her mouth wider, tilting her neck to the side so he could move deeper. His tongue explored her mouth, a singing desire like a wasp held between his teeth, and its sting was both venomous and beautiful. She moaned again as his hand moved up under her T-shirt and pressed against the naked mound of her breast, causing her to pull her hands behind her neck. Nathan grinned as she pulled her shirt the rest of the way over her head.

Both of her breasts swam out and deflated against her thin chest. As she inhaled, her ribs gleamed in the light with their own shadows like the rungs of a ladder leading all the way down to the obtuse angle of her hip bones. She swallowed and strained against a fresh spasm of desire as his mouth went lower, searching the skin of her neck and down her breastbone, until it trailed across one nipple. Nika quaked, opening her eyes and looking down as he moved his lips across it, and it hardened under the gentle circular caress of his tongue.

“Suck me harder,” she murmured. He smiled and went to the other breast, eliciting the same ferocious drive of passion. She clenched her other breast with her own hand, massaging it and imagining the wet dark organ of his tongue.

Nathan’s hand moved further down, slipping under her jeans, and she grunted as he pulled up gently against her groin. Her legs opened automatically, and he pinched the tiny bead of her clitoris through her panties, massaging it up and down between the gaps in his fingers.

“Uhhn, Nathan,” she turned her head against the pillow.

“Yes?” he said, moving his mouth down in tiny kisses over her navel and to the lip of her jeans where a few dark hairs marked the beginning of her pubic region. She arched her waist toward him.

“Take my pants off,” she smiled.

They crumpled onto the floor beside the couch and he moved his hands across the fabric of her panties again, pressing two fingers in against her vulva. The labial slit of her vagina darkened against the outline of the panties as he rubbed faster, and she twisted against his grasp.

Her own hand moved down, and tickled across his abdomen until she found his member stiff and hard against the waistband of his pajamas. Like a geographer, she mapped the topography of his muscles, the way his groin arced down into a triangle, and fished out the heavy pale organ. As she pulled back on it and the foreskin peeled away, she found herself staring at the massive red mushroom of his penis. Overcome with a sudden urge, she tugged on it and felt it rub against her palm like a sticky and eager organism.

"Do you want to have sex?" he asked.

The answer was already obvious, but she nodded anyway, opening her legs wider as he scrambled out of the pajama bottoms and cast the bathrobe to one side. Fully naked and tethered by wiry muscles, he was like an adamantine god above her. She felt a renewed desire replenish herself like a forgotten well as he leaned over her. It was both terrifying and awesome, like standing on the edge of a precipice, tempting fate to push you over the side.

He gently pried apart the side of her panties where her vagina glistened and moved his own finger upward against the clitoral folds. He saw her shiver, the nerves in her legs tightening like winches. As he pushed apart her labia with his two fingers, she took his member in one hand and moved her waist upwards toward him. When they met, she gasped and bit down on the palm of her other hand to keep from screaming out in pleasure while Nathan's hand gripped the side of the couch as he pushed gently into her tight canal.

Slowly, they rocked back and forth. He reached down and caressed her breasts again, pushing upward. With each thrust, she closed her eyes and opened her mouth, as if the next might awaken some other animal she had let hibernate. His hands spread down across her and then gripped her waist. Her thighs opened wider, slick and strong with the acrid smell of both of them. His hands tightened on her muscles, moving inward, and he thrust again. She lifted her groin toward him and they both reveled in the act of coupling.

His penis swelled inside her, a lustrous pillar of manhood, throbbing against the walls of her vagina, and Nika began to pant like a dog, her eyes suddenly drifting into a sleepy stare. Her fingers came down to spread her vagina wider, and she stroked at the red inflamed bulb of her clitoris that peeked out from its sheath, surrounded by a tangled damp mass of thin pubic hair.

"You're so beautiful," Nathan said, breathing heavily. He pumped into her harder, causing her breasts to shake. She reached behind to grasp at the armrest of the couch, lifting her legs higher until she was splayed entirely before him.

"Love me," she pleaded, and grit her teeth, "oh god, Nathan, love me!"

He grunted and pulled out of her and she turned over and propped herself on her knees, bending her ass up into the air in invitation. She buried her own head into the pillow at an angle, and the slim rise of her spine broke out against her skin like a mountain range, something wild and unexplored in its own right. Nathan spread her legs wider as he moved towards her, his own penis dripping with her juices, and plunged into her exposed sex again. This time, she bucked and flailed as he pummeled against her G-spot.

Nika groaned and begged for more, and reached between her legs where a gush of something hot exploded between her fingertips and ran down her inner thighs, flowing almost to her navel. She knew she was close, and could predict Nathan's own release, his heartbeat transmitting through the swollen organ that was crushing against her insides.

"I'm, I'm going to cum," Nathan said, gripping both sides of her waist as he entered her again in frantic motions, and closed his eyes tight. "I can't hold it!"

"Cum in me!" she screamed, her own hands clenching down on the mattress.

He butted into her hard and she squeaked in pain and surprise as he climaxed, a white hot jet that launched against her insides and she felt her knees give out as she fell forward. Her vagina rocked violently, closing and unclosing in tepid spasms as his seed leaked out of her and her own orgasm flooded through her system.

Hunched over, her face buried into the cushion, Nathan wrapped his arm over her and rubbed her back as she gasped and wracked for breath, unable to contain her own body for the overload of stimulus that rushed through her. Her lips pouted outward and she made a low growling sound as she rocked back and forth like a trauma patient. When it had finally subsided, she stretched out like a cat on her side. Nathan tucked himself in behind her, his groin like a wet cushion against her round nubile buttocks, his hand draped across both swollen breasts.

She opened her eyes and watched the room. The books on the shelves eavesdropped on them, and she felt his heartbeat again, this time through his chest pressed against her back.

"Do you recognize me now?" he asked playfully.

Nika smiled and closed her eyes. "This is the Nathan I recognize," she confirmed, "don't leave me again. Please. I don't want to be alone."

"I'll never leave you," he said.

She laughed, remembering one of the first things he'd ever told her – that a promise from him was immutable. "Is that a promise?" she asked.

He kissed her ear, and pulled a reddish-black lock of hair across her eyes. "Aye."

CHAPTER 12

Clara was visibly relieved to see Nathan return to her, though she rapped him firmly on the top of the head when he relayed the events that had happened at the village. He also spoke of the illusion he had been party to, in order to convince everyone he killed the last raider as an act of vigilant recompense.

She had grown older in the span of a few weeks as well. Nika could still remember the stern woman who had let her into their house with mixed convictions. Since then, the two had become as close as sisters, Nika thought, though never having had a sister she didn't really know what it felt like.

"You bastard," Clara said, strutting back and forth in Nathan's room where they'd convened. She'd come back a day after, but had stirred up little more information. In the wake of the slaughter of Corin's village, Nathan's rise to Alpha was now unanimously accepted.

"I'm sorry," Nathan said, and glanced at Nika, "I know I'll be making apologies for a while. But it was necessary to make everyone believe I'd gone off the deep end."

"That's what I don't get… why?" Nika said. She was sitting cross-legged on the couch, and put on a slim nightdress that hugged her chest with the light incandescence of silk. Her long thighs perched outward askew. "Why the deception?"

Nathan hesitated again, and Clara rapped him firmly on the head for a second time. "Ow! Okay, I got it," he protested, skipping backwards. He let himself regain some composure before he spoke again. "The truth is, it was a spur of the moment decision. I don't really know what I planned to do with the raider Alex brought me… he was pretty badly hurt, could barely talk. One of Alex's guys had dislocated his jaw. But I asked him anyway."

"What?" Clara blurted.

"Who hired him to attack the camp," he said as e blood drained out of his face. "He wasn't in any condition to fight us. He must've thought he was dead anyway, so there was no point in hiding the fact or being stubborn. He told me who was behind it. His group of shifters used to be rogues, like Alex. But unlike Alex and his northern brotherhood, these were urbanites, rogue wolves trying to live in a human world. Most of them were delinquents, from what I could gather, those without a home, trying to make odds meet. Many were criminals."

"Stop stalling, Nathan," Clara warned, raising her fist again.

"I'm getting to it," he said, "The raider told me he had been picked up – by someone he called the Savior – another shifter who had recognized their plight. That humans and shifters were… inconsolably different. That peace could never exist, and things should go back to the old ways."

"The old ways had shifters hunting humans, and exiled to the northern lands," Clara responded with disgust.

"The raiders didn't see it that way. They took this Savior at his word – that he would help them reclaim their destiny by sculpting a new kingdom, one founded on the empire of humans, but ruled by wolves."

"Madness," Clara interrupted again, "such a thing is grandiose, but foolhardy. There were what, a few hundred of them? They expected to take on every single human?"

"They were desperate," Nathan shrugged, "and the promise of the Savior was too hard to resist."

"So this Savior is behind the attacks," Nika bit her thumbnail, "no wonder he wanted me dead – it all makes sense now. If a human died after going out on a date with you, Nathan, it would discredit you. An attack on humans in general would, I gather, throw all of the packs into turmoil. While they were trying to figure out who was behind it, the raiders could work behind the scenes to try and destabilize power. It also explains why they attacked the forum – an assembly of all the packs would mean the Alpha leadership would cement itself, and the raiders would lose their opportunity."

Nathan held up a finger. "Almost, but not quite. What if the forum was called *precisely* in order to gather so all the leader and elders could be routed in one fell blow, and both contestants for the next Alpha leadership eliminated as well? One single move, and you would wipe out any chance of the wolf shifter alliances being able to stand against the tides of civil war."

Clara dropped down and sat on the steps that led up to a raised dais where Nathan's bed was anchored to one wall. "Nathan, that's crazy," she said, "The forum was called by Aaron, in order to *protect* the assembly – with so many shifters, it would be suicide to try and assassinate the leaders – or you and Dean, for that matter."

"And yet, how many did we lose in the ambush?" Nathan's observation cut to the bone and Clara dipped her head in remorse. "No, the forum was the perfect opportunity – with enough shifters, with enough planning, and by waiting for the right moment, their victory would have been assured. It almost was, if not for Flores. Her prudence in enlisting Alex' group as protective custody for the forum is the only thing that prevented all of us from being wiped out."

Nika uncrossed her legs. "She saved us," the human woman remarked.

"If the forum was a trap, then…" Clara lifted the blade of her chin at her brother, and her lips pursed as a premise formulated in her mind, something she had never even considered, because it was so unspeakable, so beyond the realm of any of their imaginations, to consider.

Nathan let it drop. "There was only one person more prudent in his strategy, in his plans within the plans, than Flores – the very man who she learned that skill from. The one who knew where and when the forum was happening, who knew about the transgenic gene that Clara and I carry, the one who called the forum in the first place."

"Aaron," Nika whispered.

"I don't believe it!" Clara lashed out, anger overcoming her words, and she charged toward the door of the room and reached for the handle but couldn't bring herself to turn it. "I don't believe it."

Nathan touched Clara's shoulder. "They didn't find his body among the others," he said, "and he was an old timer wolf. He knew what things were like, before humans and wolves co-existed. He may have preached the necessity of change but there was always a sliver of doubt in his voice when he talked about it. Like he longed for the past. If he found the raiders – an unknown branch of wolves without a leader or purpose, who had fallen on the wayside of history – they would have been the perfect blank canvas for him to use to paint his own version of paradise. He used them. In the same way he used us. He probably hoped to capture either you or me for our blood."

"The transgenic gene," his sister drawled, her lips shaking, "that's how he meant to fulfill his promise to the raiders. Not by getting rid of the human population but by turning them – transforming them into shifters, like us."

Nathan nodded and stepped back, taking a seat on the couch beside Nika where he wrapped his arm around her. "This is what the raider told me: the name of his Savior, our uncle, Aaron," he said, "When he told me that, I knew that I was in over my head, and I had to keep it to myself. I pretended to dispose of his body, and had one of Alex' men bind his wounds. You also understand why I couldn't let Dean know."

Clara snarled at the warped state of affairs Aaron had thrown them into, events that cost him the life of his own daughter. "Son of a bitch!" she snarled and punched the doorframe so hard Nika was sure her fist would go through the oak frame, "He didn't give a damn about any of us. He might as well have loosed the arrow that took Flores' life!"

Nathan gulped. He knew Clara's temper was on the same level as Dean's when he got angry, and didn't point out that was one of the reason's he'd waited until now to tell her, as well. "If Dean knew, I don't know what he'd do."

"He'd bloody well run into the woods and harangued his snout for his father's own blood until he found it," Clara spat in a crisp sentence, "and so would I. You did the right thing, Nathan." The strength left her and she reached for the door handle again and put her forehead against it. "What the hell…"

Nathan continued. "I've been in contact with Alex' group the last couple of days. The raider recovered, somehow. Leave it to northern rogues to know how to tend their wounded."

"He's *alive*?" Nika gasped.

"For now," Nathan said, unflinching, "I ordered him to be let go, and to return to his master."

"After he already betrayed him to you?" Clara gaped.

"I don't think he thought he'd survive his own wounds," Nathan said, "but there's nowhere else for him to go. If any of the villagers or other wolf packs find him, he's dead. His only choice is to return to his own pack, and to Aaron. With a message."

Clara let go of the door handle and leaned against it, sinking down until her knees were against her chest. Her little brother wasn't so little anymore. She looked exhausted, but also proud, an inconceivable contradiction of emotions that she had given up trying to reconcile. *Like so many of us*, Nika thought.

"What message?" she queried.

Nathan beamed. "Just three words, and a location," he said, "I thought I'd keep it short. Didn't want any misunderstandings, and given the condition of the messenger, I wanted to be sure he'd deliver it before Aaron dispensed his own punishment."

Nika shivered. *Three words.*

"Wolves deserve wolves," Nathan replied.

*

Outside, a harsh grey ribbon of weather was prevailing on the border between the prairies and the Rocky Mountains, slamming against the stony spines like torrential airborne waves. There was electricity in the air, a palpable energy eroded into the atmosphere, scattered like leaves. Every so often, it would bundle itself into a lightning strike and punch the earth to the north where the horizon was cloven between sharp mountains and the empty liminal curve of the earth.

Aaron counted under his breath, and when he reached six, a boom echoed over the corrugated tin of the cabin's roof. He leaned back in the old rocking chair and tapped the end of his cigarette against the side of the battered off-green wooden table, blackened by age. Ash dripped and diffused onto the floor, and he inhaled again and blew smoke out of his curled white-whiskered lips.

Out the window, rain plumes slanted downwards, and he frowned. There was a scream out back, muffled by a well-timed crack of thunder that issued south and shook the windowpanes. He felt a sour taste invade his mouth, like he'd taken a bite of something that wasn't ripe yet – *maybe that's not far from the truth*, he thought peevishly.

He had tried to plan everything accordingly, to account for every contingency. *Pride is a poor substitute for patience*, he thought wearily, and rubbed his brow where his whitened hair drooped down his back and tapped his cigarette against the table again. Maybe he was getting too old, or else he had simply underestimated his enemies but the consideration of the latter was another bitter flavor he couldn't swallow and he spat onto the floorboards, as if it might clear his palate.

There were things he hadn't expected. Flores, for one, and he regretted that – truly, he did. She shouldn't have had to die, and that was an oversight he had taken personal liberty to rectify. The shifter who had lodged an arrow in her belly had already met a similar fate. *But a shame, nevertheless*, he thought. Still, it had been her own fault. She had ruined what had otherwise been a perfect setup; the northern rogues had killed almost all of the raiders he had militarized and enlisted, and those who remained had their faith shaken to the core by seeing their numbers dwindle to such a handful.

"I'm not finished yet," he scowled out the window to the thunderheads, and stood up, his knees creaking with the effort. He yearned for his wolfish form again – at least as a wolf, he was strong. Not like this feeble human illusion. He hated his wrinkled hands, the detriment of dotage.

He couldn't shake an impending fear, though. He limped to the door and stepped outside, pulled up the collar of his jacket against the chilly gust of air and scanned the horizon. Near a small tree gathered several of the raiders, all of them young, skittish. A rope was hanging from one branch, and attached to it, a body swung like a metronome. What was that old phrase? *Don't kill the messenger.*

Aaron felt a sick laugh twist in his gut, but kept it clamped down inside his throat as he joined the throng of shifters who were all staring at the ground – none of them had the heart to look up at the bloated face of one of their own. *Just like Nathan*, the old wolf thought. The new Alpha's single message, transmitted via the corpse now dangling in the air, his feet pointed down at the earth and eyes still goggled and wide, aiming at the sky, had told Aaron all he needed to know.

"He means to undo me," he said, "and now he knows whom he's dealing with."

He took a small degree of smug satisfaction, trying to imagine his and Clara's face when he'd found out who had sold them out. Humans and wolves, together? He spat again on the grass, and one of the raiders shriveled in fear. *I should've killed the human whelp outright*, he thought, remembering how hard it had been to put on a genial mask of acceptance for her benefit.

"Your brother," he shrugged, trying to cover the segue of his own thoughts blurted out loud, "he was not strong. Not as strong as you are! He failed because he didn't believe in me – in our cause!"

Aaron's booming testament was on par with the distant thunder and its effect on the huddled mass of pitiable shifters with downcast glares was equable. Just as they refused to look into the face of the hanged man, they could not bear to meet the gaze of their leader, their Savior.

"He betrayed us all," Aaron continued, forcing sadness into his voice, "and for that, his punishment here is just. He died as one of us, but he had to die. You will understand this, in time. But we cannot tarry now! We must be emboldened by his sacrifice, otherwise he will have died in vain, and we must carry his memory as our banner.

"I can see it in your faces. You want revenge for your fallen brothers. Well, so do I! Fear not, my brothers, you will taste their blood soon enough. But we must make preparations. Do not hang your heads in sadness, but look to the new dawn. Our new world *will* be there… hold that in your hearts."

Aaron saw a smoke-thin tract of hope enter into the faces of some of the raiders, and knew he was on the right track. He tried to prop himself up straight and nodded at them all in turn. "Our world waits for us, brothers. Will you help me grasp it?"

At this, a jubilant cry rang out, and determination forged by loss and hatred steeled the young shifters, and even Aaron felt a chill, something not born of thunderstorms or winter air but a far less tangible force. He smiled and prepared for his finale.

"Then sing, brothers! Sing for the vengeance we will wreak on any who stand in the way of our glorious future. Let us fight our way back into the light. The other packs will tremble at our power, and when they ask for mercy," he paused again, just long enough to bring a momentary silence to the crowd who shushed synchronously and craned forward, their eager faces daring to believe in the Savior's words, "we will stand above them and cry out in one voice: *wolves deserve wolves!*"

At this, chaos broke out and all of them raised their heads and began to howl. Some of them tore at their clothes, shredding fabric as they clambered into their nakedness, and began to transform into wolves. But without exception, each of them tipped their heads back at the angry sky and howled. It was not elegant, not beautiful, Aaron thought, not like the sort of call that was allotted for the ceremonies of death and the celebration of a departed soul. This was dissonant and pierced, an abject fury tumbling headlong on its own momentum.

Aaron smiled, satisfied with his speech, and marched back into the cabin and shut the door. Outside, he could hear them still singing and carousing. *Let them sing*, he thought, remarking on how fitting Nathan's singular message to him had been in captivating the trust of his brood once again. He fingered another cigarette from the carton and discovered it was his last. He hadn't smoked in years, ever since he and the children had parted ways.

It seemed somehow fitting to start again. He missed the taste of smoke in his lungs, the masochistic burn of it searing against his insides, as if to remind that he was, in fact, still alive. It was so easy to forget, in this human form but he needed it a little while longer. The Savior was human-shaped, after all.

The coal of the cigarette glowed and sizzled and he

leaned back in the rocking chair again, gnawing on his tongue, and licked his lower lip. Somewhere across that empty expanse, out the window, where the indistinct orange glow of Calgary burned against the horizon, Nathan was probably staring at the same slate grey sky.

"So you mean to meet me head on, do you, young pup?" he thought, amused again by his nephew's message. The raider he had let go had also mentioned a location before Aaron had struck him hard against the side of the temple with his own fist, and how fitting! He took another deep inhale and saw the cigarette was already down to the filter. With a flick of his finger, he cast it towards the window again.

Just beyond the eye, covered now by storms raging in from the north and Chinooks rattling their rains across from the west, was an occluded spire of blue granite. A place he knew well, a place from his youth, which was so long ago now, and yet his memory of it was still crystal clear as the waters that ran off it from deep nested and eternal glaciers.

The Jaw.

"How fitting," he murmured again with a twinkle in his eye, but his mouth sagged to one side, and he reached for another cigarette, having forgotten the carton was empty. "Bad habits die hard," he said to himself, and wondered just what he meant by that.

CHAPTER 13

"I've thought about it a lot. I thought about at least once an hour, after I first met you," Nika said. Nathan was lying beside her again, the two were huddled under the sheets. "I thought to myself, 'just turn around, Nika, you can go back to your old life right now'. But the more I thought about it, the more I realized I didn't have an old life anymore."

Nathan breathed against her neck, causing the thin wisps of her hair to curl over and flutter, and she giggled and turned to face him. His hand stroked her cheek softly, and his blue ermine eyes rested motionless against her lips. "Then what happened?" he urged quietly.

"Then everything happened," she smiled, "and you happened. I can't go back now, Nathan. I've wanted to tell you for a while now, but I couldn't ... couldn't bring myself to do it because I wasn't sure about how I felt, if what I was feeling was real or just … adrenaline, heh. And I didn't know how you felt about me."

He bent and kissed her on her lips. "You do now?"

"No," she laughed, "No, I don't know. I'm taking a leap of faith. Something I should have done a long time ago – maybe in his quirky way, James knew something like this would happen when he gave me the address to that dating website."

"I'll have to meet your roommate one of these days,"

Nathan replied wryly, and blew on her nose until she blinked and giggled again. "I'm picturing an old wizened guy who smokes a long hand-carved pipe made of ebony or something."

This time, Nika laughed for real and it chimed against the ceiling. "He's skinny, balder than the tires on my car, and takes pride in developing new and interesting daiquiris for when I get home from work," she replied, trying to paint a picture.

Nathan scrunched his eyes, pretending to imagine him. "And handsome?"

She touched his cheek in a mock slap. "Not like you," she chided, "Why, are you jealous of my gay roommate?"

He shrugged and pushed out his lower lip. "Before, I might've been … he got to see you every day," he said in earnest, and she smiled and kissed him back. He turned over on his back and she wrestled her face closer to his chest while they watched the ceiling fan.

"You're going to meet him, aren't you?" she asked, her voice muffled by his sweater.

He touched her head, slid his fingers against her scalp. "I have too, Nika," he crooned, but his voice was tense, pulled in too many directions by words like *duty* and *obligation*, and she knew there was nothing she could do to sever his ties from them. They were as intrinsic to his role as Alpha as his wolf-form was to him.

"Not just for what he's done," Nathan continued, unabated, "although that's part of it. I owe it to Flores to hold him accountable, and to Corin and his village. He's still out there, and even if we managed to foil his plan, Clara or I won't be safe until he's put away. I mean to end this, Nika, oncc and for all."

"At what cost," she half-whispered.

He couldn't answer her, and again they lapsed into silence. "That old life you were talking about," he said "the one you thought you couldn't go back to. I think you're wrong. Just because you met me, doesn't mean that your whole existence has to change. My world has grown dangerous, Nika, more dangerous than I've been willing to admit."

She propped herself on her elbow and looked at him with circumspect wariness, sensing another shift in him. "What are you getting at?"

He tried to smile. "I mean I don't want you here," he said with a straight face, "not while the threat of Aaron is still out there. You need to try and go back to your old life. At least for now."

"What are you saying?!" she said, pushing herself off the bed. She had thought she'd lost him once before to his own private darkness, but to lose him again out of some misguided sense of trying to protect her was too hard to accept. "We started this together," she fumed, "we end it together, Nathan. I don't care about the danger – we're stupid together like that. Think about how you would feel if our positions were reversed. You can't just abandon me, you promised you wouldn't!"

He reached out and hugged her, even as her arms curled up against her chest. "Nika, I'm not abandoning you," he said, "far from it. But these are *shifters* we're dealing with – humans are no match for them. To bring you along now would endanger you needlessly. Surely, you see that."

She stopped fighting him momentarily and her nostrils flared with frustration. Yes, she could see the logic but it didn't make it any easier to swallow. "So I go back to my gallery and look at art and pretend you and Clara aren't out there, fighting for your lives?" she said assertively.

Nathan held both her wrists, brought them up to his mouth, and kissed each. "No," he said, "you go back to your gallery, and you forget about everything, and when I come back – and I will – you and I will go on that date we promised."

"You make a lot of promises," Nika reproached.

"And have I broken any of them yet?"

Her cheeks flushed and she pulled her arms away but remained sitting in front of him. The candle on the windowsill wavered as a fragmented ghost of wind picked at it like an orange scab.

"No," she replied, "and you'd better not start."

*

Clara adjusted her leather jacket. There was a clean tear running at a sharp angle under her right arm and across her back from a scuffle in the ambush. She had sewn it back together herself with black thread, and there was something ominously Frankenstein-esque about her appearance. She had cut her hair as well, trimming the back into a comparably sharp angle and leaving her bangs long. *For Flores*, she said, when Nathan had tentatively asked about it.

"You look scarier than normal," he commented, swinging his leg across the Ducati in their underground garage. The last time he'd used the bike had been when he'd dropped Nika off on their first date. *Full circle*, he mused.

Clara knocked her helmet across her knees and made an effort to toss her bangs back across her shoulders. "Hopefully Aaron and his bastard-born lackeys will think so too," she said with matter-of-fact sternness, and then pivoted her frown into a smile, "this is probably suicide, little brother."

"Let's not get ahead of ourselves," he said, slipping his helmet on and knocking the kickstand with his heel. "I have no intention of getting either us killed. I'm still counting on a diplomatic solution to all of this."

"When did you get so much older than me?" Clara wondered, "I remember when you needed help with your homework." Pride had gone back into her, and even though she knew it was selfish, it made her grin at her own reluctance to let Nathan grow up, but he had anyway, despite her best efforts to keep him safe, to protect him from an adult world she had entered before she should have had to.

He folded up his visor and combed the daggers of black hair out of his eyes. "You're going to make me blush, Clara, knock it off," he joked, "I may be Alpha of the Pack now, but that doesn't change *me.* I'm still Nathan… you're supposed to remind me of that when I lose track. I'm counting on it, okay?"

Still Nathan, Clara recollected, flipping the dark tinted shield of her own visor down, *but not the boy-child any longer.* He was a man, in whatever context that meant in their contemporary world, one at an impasse as it tried to bridge two very different and contrasting worlds under a single paradigm of symbiotic unity.

"Are you worried?" she asked, trying to change the subject and clicking her boots onto the pedals of her own bike, a hyped-down version of his own Ducati. "About Nika," she clarified, and then regretted bringing it up. It had been hard enough for the two of them to separate, and right now, Nathan needed all of his focus on Aaron. "Never mind," she added hastily.

He tapped his helmet. "I made her a promise I'd come back," he said, "I intend to honor it."

Without another word, he kicked the clutch and cranked the throttle, tearing out of the garage with a squeal of rubber, and Clara pulled back on her own and followed after. *So be it,* she thought. They made it onto the Trans-Canada highway in five minutes and steered west, taking advantage of the straight-as-an-arrow stretch of road to push their bikes to the limit. The whine of both engines following one after the other was shrill, a banshee of pistons and gasoline, and seemed to mime the pursuit of two wolves, each carrying the other's pace as they made for the saw-tooth kerf on the horizon.

The Jaw was a perfect example of how unrelenting the earth could be in its digestion of stone and usurpation of the landscape. It was a place Aaron had first introduced him to, saying the mountain had a lesson for him. Now Nathan understood at least a facet of that unspoken tutelage: *the necessity of patience*. Aaron had demonstrated it with his elaborate plan to take control of the Pack and start his own revolution on humanity. Nathan would have to demonstrate it now if he hoped to prevent it.

The siblings dropped their bikes at the gravelly turnout and trekked south over the creek. Soon, they were in the haunting blue-green fragrance of pine trees, the sweet smelling sap of conifers. They moved lightly, all their senses open and available to the world around them for the slightest change, whether it was shift in the wind or the snap of a branch. At the base of The Jaw, where the terrain suddenly arched upwards between muskeg and huge lichen-covered boulders, they saw the shale and granite scree slope tilting up toward the face of the summit.

Clara blinked against a gust of wind, and followed Nathan as he marched toward a discernible animal path switch-backing up the slope. "Something's in the wind," she murmured.

"I know," he said over his shoulder. His Kevlar jacket caught the heavy folds of his hood and pressed it against his neck as he continued to climb up the slippery rocks. Small avalanches of stones cascaded down under his feet. "Aaron's waiting for us. Be careful, Clara. He's lost everything and that makes him desperate – everything we think we know about him can't be trusted. At this point, we can't afford to think of him as our uncle anymore."

"I stopped thinking of him as family," she barked, "but thanks for the warning."

"You're my backup," he smirked and looked down at her, offering a glove hand with the fingers cut off. She grabbed it and he pulled her up onto the switchback trail. "Just want to make sure when things go sour, you don't hesitate."

He made to pull his hand back but Clara held it firm until he looked back at her questionably. "You're all I got, idiot. I'm not going to falter," she murmured and punched him in the arm. "Let's go say hello to Aaron."

By time they reached the top of the plateau, they were both winded, but they made an effort to stand still. Nathan's legs were burning but the climb infused his nervous system with adrenaline, for which he was thankful. The stench of other shifters inundated the small bench of the moraine. Clara held her nose against the wretched fog of uncleanliness that even the wind couldn't sweep away, and pointed toward a small sliver of stone that had long ago peeled off the sheer rock face above them. Clouds swam over the top, overlaid against the cobalt sky, with the swiftness of a time-lapse, and Nathan looked away quickly to avoid a sense of vertigo.

"Hello, pup," croaked a familiar voice, and Aaron appeared from behind the sliver, his hands deep in the pockets of a black coat that could easily have been as old as him. His white whiskers had started to grow out and they frosted his cheeks like sleet. "You're looking well – like a real Alpha."

"Glad you got my message," Nathan replied. There was no sign of other shifters but the small hairs on the back of his neck tingled with the eerie sensation of being watched. There were eyes among the boulders, waiting for a command from Aaron. "Flores is dead."

"I know," he said, and nodded too many times, "that shouldn't have happened; no one regrets it more than me, Nathan, she was my own blood. I don't care if you believe that or not. But I can't bring her back, any more than I can go back now. I can't let you stand in my way."

"Is that why you tried to kill us?" Clara offered.

"Kill you? No, Clara, I wanted you to join me. To usher in a new age, where our kind would be welcome, where we could rule with impudence. A chance to reclaim our destiny… oh, you would have been a queen. You and Flores both," Aaron shouted, and his eyes took on a sheen of madness, as if he was staring out through his own delusions, trying to fit the world into a mold of his own degenerate invention.

"It's over now, Aaron," Nathan replied, "you've lost."

"And you, Nathan! I wanted you, especially. You and I could rule together! Think about it, you're the Alpha now, there's no need for us to fight, no need for more blood to be spilled. Please, nephew. Make the decision your parents should have made!" the old wolf pleaded.

Nathan froze. The death of his parents seemed like so long ago, and he had compartmentalized his grief, knowing that one day in the future there would a place for it. But to hear Aaron bring them up again, it couldn't be a coincidence. Clara must have sensed it too, and took a step forward. Nathan put his arm out, blocking her path, and felt her exhale slowly, taming a rage that was contingent on a hidden truth.

Please no, Nathan thought.

"What do our parents have to do with any of this?" the young Alpha asked warily.

Another chill ran up his spine as Aaron composed himself and took his hands out of his pocket, reaching in his coat and bringing out a carton of cigarettes. He pushed one between his lips and huddled his palms around a lighter as he lit it. "They never realized your potential, Nathan. They thought your gift was a curse, something to hide away, something to keep even from the two of you. They held you back, and tried to bury your legacy," Aaron coughed, "but I knew better. I always knew what you were capable of, Nathan, always you – so much more than my own offspring."

"What happened to our parents?" Clara snapped between clenched teeth.

Aaron glared at her. "They would've led us into ruin, into a world in which we would slowly begin to lose ourselves, our ways. I pleaded with them but they were stubborn, as stubborn as the two of you. They had to go," he said.

Nathan remembered the night Clara had come home, shaken and drenched in tears, with the news of their parents' deaths. A traffic accident, of all things, it hardly seemed possible, but now as their uncle whispered smoke from between his lips and stared them down it all began to crystallize. Clara snarled low in her throat, a guttural croak of pain and anguish, and she wrenched free from Nathan's grip and sprinted toward the old man.

Aaron snapped his fingers, without looking up, and half a dozen raiders suddenly emerged from their hidden vantage points, their grey cloaks swirling about them and snapping taut in the wind that cart-wheeled over the flat bench. Nathan launched forward after his sister even as the shifters converged on her, and he met one head-on. The Alpha dodged a clumsy fist and brought his own fist up against the wooden mask, shattering both it and the face behind. A second shifter grabbed Nathan from behind in a bear hug and squeezed so tightly he was afraid he might've snapped a pair of ribs. Gasping, he swung his head backwards and heard another crack of cartilage and a stifled groan. Bringing his elbow up, he collided with the attacker and felt the arms slacken on his sternum as he connected with an undefended temple.

Nathan lodged another kick into the ribs of the second attacker, but was too slow when a third shifter caught him in the abdomen with a roundhouse kick. Air flashed out of his lungs like a vacuum in space, and he felt a heavy pressure connect with his chest as his vision blurred into a frenetic montage of blue sky, and the earth loomed up again as he hit a flat stone. Through a numb pain, he looked up and saw Clara almost make it to Aaron.

Before she could rip into their uncle, however, two more shifters staggered into her path. One of them was fully in wolf form, and his huge shaggy grey complexion arched like a bow of flesh and tendon, ready to spring. It didn't stop Clara in the least as she dove head-first toward her attackers. The wolf closed its jaws at her with a terrifyingly wet snap like someone wringing a towel, but it found only empty air. Clara launched into the air, stepping off the overcast collar of the wolf and flipping over its back in a twisting handspring. She landed just in time to duck a blow from the second shifter, who swung a heavy broken branch at her head – the wood whistled over her as she pivoted on one heel and brought her legs around in a circular arc, taking out his knees.

The shifter grunted as he fell down to her level, and staggered back as she planted her foot into his face. A deep crack ran up the wooden mask and he hovered there, his muscles still supporting his weight even though he was seeing stars. Clara finished him off with a second kick, her heel catching him high under the chin. He coughed and clutched at his neck as he fell onto his back with a mute thud, and blood sputtered up through the crack in his mask as he nursed his shattered windpipe.

Then she was up again, and moving toward Aaron, who still stood irresolute and immobile as a gargoyle, a stony look glassed on his face as his cigarette coaled brightly and smoke bathed his face like undulating rivers of charcoal blue. *Almost there*, she thought, reaching out toward him, her hand strained into a claw.

Pain jetted up her right leg and she gasped as her momentum was cut short. Her body tightened like a slack rope suddenly stretched out on either end, and then she was moving backwards. The wolf she had managed to somersault over had turned around and clamped its teeth shut on her lower calf – she looked behind her in terror, time seeming to slow to a trickle, as she perceived the superfluous hate and malcontent of the beast that had pinned its teeth into her. There was another surge of pain and a dizzying movement as the wolf shook its head and flung her through the air, and for a moment, she perched on an invisible balance of air.

A desperate wheeze. The gravel and sharp plated shale rose toward her and she closed her eyes. There wasn't pain this time, only a terrific dance of lights and the sensation of a great force bleeding into every muscle and nerve, and she let out a sigh as she spun across the flat bench and came to a rest on her side. She groaned, and turned her head. Her vision fluctuated through a red prism, and she saw her right leg strewn out under her, useless and sodden with blood that stained her pant leg black. Her pulse rung in her ears, and pulsed in the wounded appendage. *How useless*, she thought, with a wry sort of terror that was part acceptance. *This is how it ends, then*, she lamented, and looked for her brother.

She could hear her name coming from somewhere. But it was so far away, and her vision was now closing around a tunnel of blackness, pulling her farther from the voice. She smiled again, and let her head go limp.

"CLARA!" Nathan shouted, scrambling toward her.

Her eyes were closed and she had a pitiful smile on her lips. Blood had trickled down her forehead and across one eye where it had pooled and then ribboned down her cheek. Nathan snarled, spittle foaming at his lips, and he crouched on all fours, putting himself between the remaining shifters and his sister.

The first raider to make it to him was the unluckiest. Nathan leaped forward, burying both knees into his chest, and brought his hands down again and again on the man's unprotected head, gouging his eyes and flattening every recognizable feature. It took less than a second for the raider to fall onto his back with Nathan on top, but he was dead by the time he hit, blood and cerebrospinal fluid squashed together in a ruddy mixture.

"Come on!" he shouted, looking for death.

The other raiders hesitated for a moment but Aaron snapped his finger again, and like some stoic Pavlovian trick, they roared in unison and collided on top of him. Fists and feet pummeled at Nathan as he fought to stay conscious. He didn't even feel the punches after a while, just the sounds of their knuckles tenderizing flesh, and spat and screamed at them in futility. Another well-aimed fist took him across the temple and he felt the earthquake under him, a swelling of nausea deep in the bowels of his stomach. Expressionless wooden masks glared at him, but the eyes behind them were laced with resentment and with a misguided and perverted cruelty. *The hunt, which has become the slaughter*, Nathan managed to think, and closed his eyes.

Thunder rang out across The Jaw, echoing off the metaphorical fangs of granite. He opened his eyes again. Clouds split against its high steeple and parted like water breaking against the bladed side of a paddle. More thunder, right on top of the first, a hollow echoing sound issued like the crack of a whip. A third – no, that was impossible – and even through the blurriness of pain and exhaustion Nathan knew thunder was not thunder at all. A chemical tang burnt the air, overshadowing even the stench of the shifters on top of him.

A fourth, and this time, the hands around the collar of his Kevlar jacket peeled back and there was a horrendous scream. More blood, not his own, splashed against Nathan's eyelids and he blinked it away, unable to understand its origin. Forcing whatever strength he had left into his legs, he sat up and saw two of the shifters splayed over, open wounds cascading blood onto the stones. The third was crawling away, dragging behind the shredded weight of his leg which had been torn apart by buckshot. He turned, as if in a daze, toward a figure near the edge of the bench. She had something in her arms, charcoal grey, tubular.

Nathan shook his head, trying to refocus his eyes. "Nika," he murmured, struggling to one knee.

Recognition flared between them, and he apprehended a smile, thin and conspicuous, but marred by the horror of what she had done in the name of her love for a shifter. The heavy shotgun in her arms streamed a hair-thin thread of smoke and she lowered it.

"Nath—"

Blood launched itself into the air in a clean swipe, splattering against the scree, and Nathan's face broke into a thousand shards, each sharper than the last. A massive dire wolf crunched down on her midriff, sinking dagger-like teeth deep inside. Its white coat was the color of clouds, off-white and coarse, and its muzzle was a massive trap of bright pink gums and stained yellow teeth. Nika opened her mouth to scream but only a dark stream pursed from her lips and her eyes widened in shock.

Aaron, in wolf form, turned his yellow gaze toward Nathan, and there was a recalcitrant accusation in those lupine eyes – *you brought her into this, now you will watch her die*, he seemed to say. He opened his jaws slowly, and more blood fountained out of the puncture wounds on Nika's stomach as she dropped the rifle and it clattered across the gravel.

"No," he choked.

The dire-wolf circled Nika's body and tilted its head. Nathan shook his head again and ran forward, even though his body felt like a broken architecture of bones and bruised muscle. Aaron was waiting for him. *The patience of the mountain*, Nathan thought, the mental image of the jaw standing out in the back of his mind like a double-negative. Patience, the one edge that Aaron had had over all of them, the ability to bide his time, the endurance to perceive the most opportune time, and then to seize it just before the door slammed shut.

Nathan ran faster.

There was one chance, and only one chance, and it was quickly closing. There was no way he could match Aaron wit for wit, and the old wolf knew that.

My only chance is to do something that he wouldn't expect, he thought, and dug his feet into the gravel again trying to pick up as much speed as possible. His eye flashed toward the fallen shotgun just beside Nika, and he screamed again, wrecking his throat with every last gasp of air.

Aaron seemed to smile as his black lips flensed back over his teeth and his snout became a ridge of bumps. Nathan leapt forward, just as the wolf tried to bite him out of the air – he could feel the shadow of the huge shifter's head blot out of the sun for a moment, the hairs under his chin scraping against the back of his jacket. In a single instant, he rolled onto the discarded gun and grabbed it with both hands. As he completed his roll, he turned, covering Nika's body with his own, and pulled back on the trigger.

The gun bucked in his hand, and sparks flew out of the casing. There was a solid thud, like someone hitting a pillow with his or her fist, and the sun returned, blinding Nathan. He shielded his eyes with his hand and saw Aaron flop over on his side, struggling to right himself. His hind leg was a stark red against the white pelt, and there was a howl of pain as he glared at his nephew.

Nathan cocked the gun and aimed again, leveling his eyes down the barrel. The second shot pinged off the gravel at Aaron's feet as the dire wolf scrambled away, barely avoiding the shot that burst dust into the air. Then he was gone. Nathan panted, squinting through one eye – there was only the sound of distant scree tumbling down the bank.

He dropped the gun. All around him, the bodies of the raiders were sprawled in a tableau of pain, and the smell of death was ubiquitous. He clutched at his mouth and turned back to Nika – her face was pale and white, and he remembered Flores the moment she had died, that same stricken look, peaceful and serene. *No, not like this*, he said, scooping her up into his arms. Her eyelids fluttered and she opened her mouth to speak as he wiped away the blood flecked on her lips.

"I… I'm sorry," she said, "you told me… to stay away. But I couldn't. I wanted to help you. I wanted to save you, like you saved me."

"You did save me," he said, and put his hand against the wound in her belly. A wetness flowed between his fingers and she let out a squeal of rending pain as he tried to stop the bleeding. "You got yourself a scratch," he said, trying to sound cheerful.

She reached up with her hand to brush away tears nearing the sides of his eyes. "I think… I may have to take a rain check… on that date you promised me."

"No, no," Nathan cried, rocking her gently, "stay with me, Nika. Don't go, please, stay with me."

"It's so dark," she said, amazed.

"Nika!" he hollered, half-sobbing into her breast, "NO!"

She closed her eyes and her head lolled back, and he

screamed again, pulling her into his own chest. He reached for her pulse, found only the faintest murmur, like something slowly echoing out. There was nothing he could do but watch, and he buried his fists into the earth, punching the shale as if he might usher life back into her by exacting penance on the mountain itself. *Nika, you can't go*, he thought, with such bland calm that he knew did not belong to him.

"You can't go," he smiled.

There was a scratching sound to his side and he whirled and saw Clara pulling herself. Her leg was badly mauled, and her pant leg was drenched, but there was a grim determination in her eyes. She had torn off her black T-shirt and wrapped it around the raider bite on her leg like a tourniquet, and shuffled her leather jacket back on, unzipped all the way. The shadows of her breasts were coated with granite dust and with her own bloody fingerprints.

"Clara," he cried, "I thought… I thought I lost you."

"Not yet, little brother," she groaned, and pulled herself toward him. He reached out, helping her toward him across the stones and she leaned against his arm gratefully. Nathan kissed her forehead and began to cry again, holding Nika's head in his lap. "It's not over, Nathan. She… hell, she's one of a kind, you don't just let someone like that go."

"It's too… too late," the Alpha stammered, his hand still clutching her belly. Nika's face was angelic in the high alpine light, and her skin had taken on a diaphanous element. "Oh, god."

"No," Clara said, pinching his shoulder with her hand, and hissed as she straightened her bad leg out in front of her, "it's not *over*." There was some hidden meaning in her words, and Nathan stared at her, lost against whatever it was she was trying to tell him. "Remember, what Aaron told us – we're special, Nathan. We're special because we carry the transgenic gene."

"What are you—"

"A shifter's regenerative ability is ten times that of a normal human," she gasped, "I'm going to pass out soon, so pay attention. We carry it in our blood, and in our saliva – Aaron said, a deep enough bite would cause a change in humans."

"You're talking about turning her into a shifter!" he spat. He couldn't believe that Clara of all people was suggesting something so abominable. Nika groaned again and went into a spasm in his arms, her mouth open and eyes rolling back in her head, and was still again.

Clara's face was a wretched knot of blood and one eye peered out through a halo of dried blood. "I'm talking about saving her, Nathan," she said.

Nathan looked at the woman in his arms – beautiful, curious, loyal. He had come to love her without ever questioning why. Like everything that happened to him, it was another event out of his control, something he could only bear witness to and participate in, without ever being an agent in its outcome. *But now I have the choice*, he thought, *to take control and make a difference – my own will, not Aaron's, not the Packs, only mine*.

Clara passed out against his shoulder and he laid her down carefully beside Nika. Grunting, he managed to stand up, and unzipped his leather Jacket. His shirt and his pants followed, crumpling to one side, until he stood naked above them. Bruises and cuts surrounded his body like a tapestry, and he could taste bile flooding the back of his throat where internal injuries had punctured blood vessels, shaken cartilage loose, fractured bones. Nathan closed his eyes and pictured a wolf in the back of his mind, a true form, the oldest legacy he had been beaqueathed. He focused on it, letting its ancient powers pulse in time with his heart.

He curled over and black fur rose on his limbs, even as they stretched outward. Fingers evolved into paws, and he raised his neck, vertebrae cracking as they realigned, until he was a dire wolf again. He limped forward, sniffing at the bodies before him. Gently, he leaned down, and with infinite care balanced one precarious fang over the puncture in Nika's stomach. She didn't react at all as he pushed it in. Her blood lapped against his tongue, salty and warm.

After half a minute, he pulled his fang back out. There was no blood from the wound this time, but a sickly purple had bloomed into the surrounding tissue. He licked the wound carefully with his large tongue and circled both the women he loved, a canine gesture that held perhaps some forgotten ritual, a symbolic act of protection. *The hearth.*

Satisfied, he curled his body around them, his tail and paws spread out like a cape. Wind howled over his fur, cold and biting, the merciless anger of the weather taunting him to give up. He only dipped his snout and whined. Nika and Clara disappeared under the warm expanse of gray fur and Nathan let out a single sigh and closed his eyes.

He would wait. Forever, if need be. But he would wait, with all the patience of The Jaw yawning above him, until both of them were returned to him. And if they did not wake, he resolved, then neither would he.

CHAPTER 14

The dream was one he didn't recognize as a dream. The edges of it were too clean, too well represented by the curvature of memory, until he realized it was, in fact, a memory – singed by adolescence, filtered through the experiences of childhood, but a memory nonetheless. It started with the smell of hay. Sweet, well-turned, a kind of musty odor that reminded him of barns and cattle and the svelte oily bodies of horses.

Sunlight came down through the dark rafters and he opened his eyes. Dust caught in the slanted light, which peered through cracks in the boards of the roof seemed to hover there, imagining itself a solid sort of substance. *What is this place,* Nathan thought, and saw himself as a boy lying on the ground, surrounded by loose yellow straw.

Laughter streamed into his ears and he turned, looking for its owner. His younger self sat up, called out though there was no sound, like the volume had been turned down on his avatar, and Nathan watched as his small legs carried him out of the barn. The empty rolling hills of Alberta stretched into incomparable distances, glancing light off their golden surfaces. The sky was mythic in its proportions, and then he heard the laugh again – Clara was giggling, and grabbed the young Nathan by both arms and they began to swing in a circle, her giddy excitement rising with tremulous notes, and her brother closed his eyes.

She used to smile so easily, Nathan thought, watching the strange image of himself playing with his sister, who couldn't have been more than ten or eleven. Her beautiful black hair was long to her waist and waved against the air like a horse's mane.

And then there were more children; Flores, skinny and awkward, joining the circle, and Dean loping behind, huge and lumbering even in his youth. Nathan felt a stab of pain, the sort that belongs to nostalgia and a conscious awareness that once certain things have lasted as long as they have, they are fated never to return. *Let me stay here*, he called out, but it was only a thought, his own voice ricocheting off the walls of his mind, *let me stay here where we were once so young, before all of it became a mess – I don't want to return.*

A rough voice muttered something and Nathan felt his vision spin around. A tall man was looking at him – not at the boy-Nathan but at *him*, as if the dream had suddenly decided to break the fourth wall.

"Father," he mouthed.

"Hello, son," he murmured. His clean cut features were just as Nathan remembered; the same lean handsome face, the trimmed and immaculate brow of hair, same balanced smile. "You're looking well."

"Why didn't you tell me?" Nathan asked.

"I wanted to protect you; so did you mother," he replied, "a parent's foolish concern, perhaps we should've told both of you. Perhaps, if we'd had more time, we would have. None of that matters now. You have to be strong, Nathan."

"I'm tired," he admitted to his father. The sky above them turned up its contrast, and when he turned, the children were gone. Only emptiness remained in the midst of grassy mounds tousled by wind. "I'm so tired."

"I know, son," his father replied, "but this isn't over. It doesn't end like this."

"How do you know?"

"I just know. Clara needs you, and so does Nika. It's time to end this, Nathan."

"I don't know how."

His father smiled. "Of course you do, you just don't want to face it," he said, "and I don't blame you. I don't envy you. And perhaps this was the real curse we gave you – not your blood, not the transgenic gene – but *this*, the burden of one day being Alpha. And all that comes along with it. But you're strong, stronger than you think you are. That's what makes you a better leader than I ever could be."

"Father," Nathan burbled, but the figure in front of him had gone shadowy, folding back into the space from whence he'd come. A distorted hand raised toward him.

"Time to wake up, son."

***

It was well into the night, when his eyes opened slowly, painfully. Stiffness ached into every joint, and he sat up, testing the muscles of his body. Strong wiry legs and arms spread out in front, as he pressed his fingers into them, trying to remember what it meant to be human again. There were tenders areas on his ribs, his arm, and his lower back, and the phantom-memory of being pummeled returned to each spot. *I'm still alive*, he remarked to himself – to recover from such a thing, he must had been in wolf form for a considerable period of time.

His eyes adjusted and he saw the outline of a fire and stood up shakily. His torso was naked, but his old cargo pants hung loosely at his ankles and drooped over his bare feet as he stumbled toward the orange glow. Deflecting glow of the coals with her open palms and face, Nika looked up at him and ran forward. *Another dream*, he thought, as she pranced into his arms and her own skinny wrists clutched at him with the mad relief of someone who had been brought back from the dead.

He felt the warmth of her tears against his chest and his own arms wrapped around her. The smell of her hair was sweet and wild as the first fragrant flowers of spring after a long winter.

"H-how…" he murmured, snapping back to reality. He squeezed her tighter against him, crushing his body into hers until she huffed to let him know he was being too rough. He relaxed, but still held her, and began to kiss her forehead and her eyelids until she giggled at him to stop. "How…"

She looked up at him, the full length of her lips red and moist. "How do you think?"

He was still reeling from the dream in which he had seen his father and he rubbed the back of his head, searching for the memory of what had happened before. He could still taste Nika's blood in his mouth, the ghost of iron and salt, and then the sound of the wind whetting itself against The Jaw of the mountain as he curled up around her and Clara.

"It's not possible," he said, but there was no other explanation. *I condemned her to a life as a shifter – as one of us*, he lamented, but rather than the forlorn and accusing expression he had expected, Nika kept smiling and shook away tears. "I'm so sorry, Nika. There was no other way. I thought… I thought I would lose you…"

"Shush," she said, and lifted a finger against his lips. "You saved me, that's all that matters."

She stepped back and pulled up the edge of her sweater. There was a gaping hole in it where Aaron's bite had gone all the way through, and it was stiff and crusty with her own dried blood, but as she exposed her belly to him, he saw that the wound had healed over entirely. There was only a small little wrinkle of a scar. She flicked it with her finger.

"Clara was just as surprised," Nika said, "she figured that whatever else your transgenic genes are capable of, they managed to increase my healing capacity several degrees beyond even you and her. I won't say it was a pleasant experience, though." She held her elbows and gulped. "I can still remember the feel of his fangs and of feeling everything drift away from me. But you were always there. That's how I found my way back."

Nathan stumbled forward again and embraced her. "Where is Clara?"

"She went for a walk around the moraine of the cliff. She wanted to see if she could pick up any traces of where Aaron had gone. He's on the run now, and without his brood of raiders, he's in a vulnerable position. I told her not to go, her leg was still badly injured, but she said she needed to move or she'd go crazy. She should be back in a few hours," Nika fidgeted, "I wanted to go with her but she told me to stay with you."

"I'm fine," he murmured.

"You weren't," Nika retorted, "You were a shelter for us for two whole days. You don't remember anything?"

He tried to scavenge through the pockets of memory that had turned themselves inside out, but it was like grasping at straws. Each time he thought he had a hold of it, it would slip between his fingers. Nathan shook his head.

"You kept us warm, me and Clara. Then you'd run down to the creek in the bottom of the valley and run back with water held in your mouth. You ran yourself almost to death trying to keep the two of us alive," her voice reached a hysterical point and she rubbed her mouth to calm herself again, "and you were just as injured as we were. You've been asleep for almost sixteen hours."

His mind was still a blank as he sat down on a bed of collected moss and cedar boughs and stared into the fire. They were on a different slope of The Jaw, this one west facing and protected from the elements by a natural scarp. Nika sat down beside him, and ran her hand along his thigh.

"How do you feel?" he asked, and she took his meaning.

"Not as different as I'd imagined," was her response, "though when I close my eyes – the moment where I fall asleep – it's like I'm being watched. It's a strange sensation; I can't explain it. Like there's another presence in my mind, something watching me from beyond the darkness, trailing along the rim of my subconscious."

"It will become easier," he consoled, "when the division starts to lessen. When you welcome the wolf into the light, you won't feel the same sort of separateness. You'll be able to co-exist."

"That's what Clara said," Nika nodded.

"You silly girl," he murmured, and pushed his fingers behind her ears, lifting her face toward him, "I will say, that was the stupidest thing you've ever done – and the coolest. Where did you get a shotgun?"

She laughed. "James' aunt is a crazy cat lady," she explained, "I told him I needed to borrow it."

"And he let you?"

Nika gave a little demure shrug. "I didn't give him the option," she remarked, and leaned toward him, tasting his lips again. He tried to say something but she clambered onto his lap, and squatted on his legs, kissing him harder until he got the hint and opened his mouth for her. Their tongues met in the liminal space between, and wrestled against one another in a moist knot. "Oh, Nathan," she murmured, clutching at the sides of his head.

"I'm here now," he said, sensing the tenseness in her voice. There had been so many moments where neither knew whether they would see the other again – *too many*, he thought. His hands moved down, settling on the top of her jeans, and he pushed his fingers under the seam where her tail-bone jutted out like a round pebble.

She crooned happily and pulled the torn sweater up over her head, her large breasts arched across her chest. Nika's lips curled in an expression of pleasure as he touched her, not with the frantic kisses that signified the other times they'd made love, but with a deliberate slowness.

His lips hovered, teasing her as he moved over her breast bone and buried his nose between her cleavage. His tongue searched for her left breast and began to lick it until goose-bumps surged across her skin. When he finally reached her nipple and planted his lips over it, nibbling it with his front teeth, she felt her abdomen swimming with desire.

Her whole body tingled with the patient progress of his mouth, and she began to pivot her hips against him, reveling in the pressure of his erection against her own groin. Her fingers moved to unzip her jeans – she wanted him inside her, for the surging and masculine breadth of his penis exploring her own luscious cave.

"Is… is horniness part of… being a shifter," she gasped through spasms of pleasure, "because I'm really horny right now. Ah, Nathan, I need you inside me… I can't wait any longer."

She clambered off his lap and they both disrobed. Then, like awkward children naked in the glow of the small fire and with the heavens wheeling above, they resumed their embrace. She put her hand on his shoulder and squatted over him, both legs straddling his own and her knees pointed outward as they faced each other. Nathan kissed her neck again and she let out a long dwindling sigh and reached down between them, fishing for his cock.

It was already rigid with his own barely contained passion, and she gasped as it enlarged against her grip. She stroked him harder until his pre-cum was slick against her palm and the wet sounds of her masturbating him had given her a tiny orgasm of her own. Propping herself up, she pushed his member between the dark folds of her labia and felt the tip of it catch at the entrance of her vagina. Another gasp as he entered her, and she opened her knees wider, trying to scoot herself down on his shaft as far her own body would permit. He probed her in sluggish pulses, raising his pelvis into her and clenching the round perimeter of her buttocks. Nika leaned against his neck and began to move her own hips, swaying them back and forth as their sexes ground together in a wet crush. The sucking of his movements in and out of her was like the hungry mouths of carp gasping at the surface of a pond.

"Unhhh, yes, please," she murmured, "yes, Nathan."

"You're so tight, Nika," he replied.

"Don't stop, don't stop," she whispered into his ear, wrapping her arms more firmly around his neck as her pale body bobbed on top.

He reached over the cleft of her buttocks, his hands plying apart both cheeks, and she felt herself widening with his girth. Her legs felt as if they were on fire, and she felt the first telltale shiver launching through her body. She jutted her hips sharply against his own, and pressed on the smooth marble-hard chest, lowering him onto his back.

His hands moved up and held her inner thighs, and she clutched at her own breasts, tweaking at the nipples as she lifted her head back. Red-black hair drooped down her back and above the top of her chest like a dark insinuation of flame, and she opened her mouth in a heavy silent scream. Her grunts were animalistic, and now she felt the wolf again – a new part of her own consciousness, trying to find the courage to come out into the open.

Nika smiled and worked herself harder against her lover, thrusting her hips in violent bursts as she gasped and groaned. Then all at once, like a thunderclap, her vagina tightened around his member and she buried her head into the pit of his neck to keep from screaming into the night air. Her legs shook with such force that she was worried she might fly off Nathan and tumble off the mountain itself.

She bit down, grinding her teeth and waiting for the climax to flush itself out of her, and Nathan wrapped his arms around her and rolled her onto her back. She pushed her legs up, folding them inward, until she was fetal with Nathan still inside her, clutched between her glistening thighs.

Shaking, she bit his ear and he smiled and looked down at her, his face centimeters from his own, a sharp dankness surrounding them and the earthy scent of their lovemaking mingling with the fresh branches under them. Her orgasm had been so intense that she hadn't even felt him come, and her hand reached down between her legs and found her pubic hair sticky and coated with his seed.

"That was amazing," she murmured, lowering her legs. Nathan's member was still half-engorged and slithered against her belly, drawing a snail's trail of clear fluid across skin. His fingers trailed across her abdomen and stopped at the small scar where Aaron had pierced her. "This is what it feels like for you all the time – how do you keep it in check?" she said in awe.

"Sheer force of will," he joked and rolled to one side.

Nika climbed across his chest again, one leg over his thigh. Her fingers lazily traced a foreign alphabet across his chest while he stared into the gallery of stars above them. "You're going after him again, aren't you?" she asked.

He grabbed her hand and kissed it. "Yes," he replied, and there was no more to say. Nika knew that it went beyond words. It was part of the *now* of wolf-thought, the collective history and rites of an ancient and noble heritage, one that demanded justice, and could not be denied by any human authority.

Am I still human, Nika thought, seeing Nathan's eyes center on the universe. It was as if the two of them were at the center, some axis mundi. *And when we step out of this moment, we will still be connected to it, through each other*, she thought, confused by the inexplicable logic of the thoughts that entered head, and seemed not to belong to her.

"I'm coming, too," she replied.

Nathan turned, and she thought for sure he would deny her again. Instead, he strained his gaze on her, and she blushed under the scrutiny, until he finally blinked and breathed out through his nose. "Wolves deserve wolves," he preached, "and now you are one."

The plainness of his comment struck her, and she swallowed, pondering the consequences of her decision. What did it mean to be a wolf? More than that, what did it mean to be the lover of an Alpha?

THE FINAL CHAPTER

Nathan and Nika had dressed again before Clara returned just before dawn, limping on her bad leg, and using a pine switch as a crutch. With a relieved gasp, she set herself down beside the dead ashes of the fire, sweating covering her face, and held up a hand before Nathan could admonish her. He knelt down beside her and swabbed her brow with the back of his sleeve.

"I know, I know," she groaned, hefting her leg out in front, "I'm a fool for taking off on my own in this condition. But you were unconscious and I needed Nika to stay here."

"You're still stupid," he replied, but his heart was filled with joy. His memory had started to return, piece by piece, and he could still clearly recall the image of her flying through the air after the shifter had chomped down on her calf. His hand shook as he wiped the grime off her face and she must have noticed because she bent forward and touched his forehead to hers.

"I'm okay, little brother," she whispered, but his hands refused to stay still until she took them in her own and laid them against her cheek. The bond between them had always been close, even if the two of them played at fighting each other at every turn. He knew that it had less to do with animosity and more to do with a shared worrying of the other. *Even as adults, we're still children,* he thought. "There's scuff-marks near the eastern rim of the jaw, just before it drops down into the other valley. I don't think Aaron wanted to risk heading back to the Trans-Canada. Most likely, he's cordoned himself off in the bowl. Sorry," she murmured, "force of habit – reconnaissance."

Nathan sniffed and found his composure again. "Then that's where we'll find him," he murmured, and motioned to Nika. "We'll be back for nightfall," he said to his sister and kissed the top of her head, "trust me to take care of this, Clara."

"I'm not coming after you this time," she said with a tone of levity, and motioned to her leg again, "just make sure you come back. Both of you."

"Promise," Nika said, straightening her back, "that means something in this family."

The sun finally cracked over the eastern horizon as she and Nathan followed the moraine, glacier carved over eons, and the smell of lichen was gritty in her nostrils. She was grateful for the new strength flowing through her muscles, and equally surprised at how her endurance had improved. Even her senses seemed heightened by the effect of Nathan's transgenic gene asserting its dominance.

She kept her fascination to herself, and trailed behind Nathan. They settled into an easygoing jaunt, and after an hour, had already made it to the far side of The Jaw, where Clara had indicated evidence of wolf.

Sure enough, even Nika was able to pick it up, though she wasn't sure what it was she was smelling until they clambered up another saw-tooth kerf of rock that pinnacled over a sharp descent.

Blood, long dried and then baked by the sun, stained the lip of the rock. Thirty feet below a shield of ice, snow combed across an inward facing bowl, pointing downward toward a glacial kettle lake which peered up at them from the surrounding meadow like an astonished blue eye.

"He must have been desperate to seek shelter down there," Nathan said, zipping up his collar, "Clara was right – he cut off his own escape. Looks like we have to jump."

Nika stepped toward the edge and looked down and felt her stomach lurch as the ground swayed in front of her. As a human, it would have been suicide, assuming they missed the outcrops of rocks hugging the cliff face and made it onto the flat slope of ice, they'd still have to deal with the fact that the glacier flowed directly into the gaping maw of the lake.

"It's okay," Nathan said, sensing her fear, and reached down to grip her hand, "don't take this the wrong way, but you don't know what you're capable of. We'll take a running start, okay?"

She didn't have the nerve to argue as he pulled her back a few feet, and then gave a nod. His arm tightened, dragging her along, and she gasped and leapt off the brink of the rock as hard as he could.

Space opened up before them like a cavity, and suddenly the two of them were rushing to fill it. Nika closed her eyes just as they impacted on the snow, and ice kicked up in front of them as they began to slide.

Nathan kept a firm grip on her hand as they spiraled, grunting with disorientation. Nika saw a sharp stone jutting out of the ice nearly take her head off and dug her heels into the snow. Beside her, Nathan did the same, and they managed to balance their descent, though they were still careening at breakneck velocity. The snow started to become softer and they felt themselves sinking into it, and then abruptly, they both stopped, a dozen feet from the cobalt edge of the lake. Nathan exhaled and collapsed on his back.

"For an Alpha, you're still as reckless as ever," Nika laughed, and helped him to his feet. Two parallel scars in the snow streaked up the slope behind them where they had first landed. Almost two hundred meters, and they'd covered it in less than a minute. *I'm really not human anymore*, she realized.

Then, across the lake, they heard a howl. Both of them whirled, ankle-deep in the slush that bit through their pant legs and socks. "There," Nathan indicated, directing Nika with his eyes toward a grove of stunted hemlock subsisting on a grassy knoll.

Aaron was still in wolf form, his body partially camouflaged by the dancing game of shadows that played through the branches of the trees. A heavy white paw, flecked with brown, splashed timidly into the artery of a small creek that wandered into the lake, and as he shifted his body toward them, it was apparent one of his legs was beyond repair. It hung behind him, flared outwards at a jutting angle, like a vestigial piece of flesh and bone.

It didn't seem to bother the shifter as he limped out of the trees as silently as a ghost, with a similar grace despite his mangled body. Two days had been enough for Clara and Nathan to recover from their injuries, but Aaron's condition had improved little. *The shotgun*, Nathan thought. Aaron had remained in wolf form and ignored the wound, hoping his shifter metabolism would take care of it. But there were still fragments of bullet buried deep inside, resting against flesh and nerves and blood vessels.

Even for a shifter of his size and disposition, the shrapnel had started to poison him from the inside out. *He's probably too far gone for us to help him*, Nathan reflected, suddenly feeling a wave of pity for the strange creature that had once been his uncle, a man and a wolf who had never been able to blend those two facets into a seamless unity.

"It wasn't within my rights to tell you not to follow me," he said, lifting his feet out of the snow and aiming for solid land several meters to their right, "but I don't know what I'm going to have to do, Nika. I had hoped… I could talk Aaron down."

"He doesn't look like he wants to talk," Nika retraced his footsteps, until they were both standing on the muddy bank. Across the way, Aaron snapped his jaws erratically, and his eyes fixated on them, both pupils dilated into huge ink drops. "But I'll let you handle him."

"Thank you," he replied, and let go of her hand as he moved slowly around the edge of the lake, never turning his back on the white dire wolf.

He remembered his dream again, a time when all of them – he, Clara, Flores, Dean, his parents – had been together. As a child, there was never any reason to assume things would ever change. Even when they did, they happened so gradually, so inexorably and without complaint, that it became impossible to gauge precisely *where* they had all drifted away from each other. *Maybe we were always meant to end up here,* he wondered, and unzipped his Kevlar jacket.

"I know you can hear me, Aaron!" he shouted at the bristling wolf, "Your raiders are dead, uncle. All of them. You're the only one who's left – so end this! Your bright world, the future you wanted to see, it's a dream, and an empty one. My parents, Corin's village, even your own daughter. How much more are you willing to lose?"

The wolf scuffed at the ground with its paws, ripping up the moss and grass mat with his claws and didn't seem to hear, or if he did, he was so far gone into his own madness and poisoned blood that the words were only sounds, barely able to scratch the surface of the animal mind he had warped into.

Don't do this, uncle, Nathan thought, but he could

already predict the old wolf's next movements. It started with a tension in the huge furred haunches, and then with blinding speed the white shape made three lunging leaps over the ground as it sought to clear the distance between its foe. Nathan was mid-transformation when Aaron's jaws snatched down inches from his own shoulder. The Alpha turned and barrel-rolled out of the way with acrobatic ease. Aaron skidded on the muddy shore and banked backward, but by this time gray fur creased over Nathan's body and his pants and jacket had ripped apart at the seams.

Nika watched in horrid fascination as both wolves faced off against each other. She had promised not to interfere, but it was easier said than done. Even wounded from the shotgun blast to his leg, Aaron was a formidable opponent, an Alpha in his own right generations ago, and proof that a true warrior didn't have to rely as much on strength as on wits. *But his wits are almost gone*, Nika consoled herself, inching closer toward the two feuding shifters, *which gives Nathan a slight advantage.*

Sure enough, Aaron seemed to be attacking wildly and without cause, wasting energy as he spun his jaws around in savage arcs. Foam sizzled between his teeth, and even from this distance, Nika could smell the rankness of death coming off his breath, something that was rotten and festering, and it made her gag. But Nathan was unshakable, his sleek gray shape dodged left and right as he retreated across the muskeg, letting Aaron wear himself out as he indulged in berserk attacks.

Finally, Aaron stopped and stood panting, his heart nearly beating out of the cage of ribs and his eyes softened, just enough for a glimmer of humanity to shine through, like a slant of sunlight through a stormy front of clouds. It was Aaron again, or whatever vestige of him was left, and he seemed to focus on Nathan with a weird recognition, as if acquainting himself with a dream suddenly condensed into reality, but still incomprehensible in its plausibility.

Yes, uncle, it is me, he wanted to say, but their wolf shapes prevented such clumsy human communication. No, Aaron knew, and the beleaguered extent of his awareness extended even to the fact that Nathan had been right. It was over, even if he was too stubborn to see it. Even if it all came crashing down to this single instance in time, Aaron came from an older era. *He means to fight it out until the end,* Nathan saw, and steeled himself for the next attack.

Aaron gave a slow single nod with his giant head, as if confirming his intention. Whatever else they were, they were shifters, and of the same blood. Nika didn't even see them charge at each other – both of them hurled over the meadow with apposite acknowledgment of the other. When they collided, it was hard enough to shake ripples into the small puddles where the fresh-water creeks pooled against the earth.

Nathan groaned and felt sharp black claws rip into his shoulder, opening up old wounds. Blood seeped down his matted pelt, and he brought his head back around to bite at Aaron. His jaws found the old wolf's collar and he sunk his teeth in and felt the satisfying spiciness of blood ring against his taste buds. He bit repeatedly, trying to open as many wounds as possible, and Aaron whined under the assault like a broken dog.

Somehow, the white wolf managed to untangle himself from Nathan's jaws and scamper back. At first, Nathan figured it was a show of defeat, but in another blur of off-white fur, the mad creature sped forward again and butted Nathan in the chest. Nathan gasped through his open muzzle and went sprawling across the bank, splashing into the shallows of the cold lake. It was like an icy bolt of lightning that shot through his whole body, and air swam out of his lungs.

Aaron growled low and limped forward, guarding him from getting back on the shore. Nathan felt his muscles cramping as he tried to maneuver past Aaron, but it was to no avail. Somehow, the white wolf had managed to find some hidden reservoir of energy and tapped into it. *A dying animal is always more dangerous than one whose life is assured*, his father had always warned, the first time he had taken Clara and Nathan hunting.

"Nathan!" Nika shouted, sensing the danger he was in, and he clicked his jaws shut in two consecutive snaps at her, as if urging her to keep quiet. Aaron turned his head very slowly toward the human on the bank, still hugging her elbows, and had a bored leer on his face.

If he finishes me off, Nathan realized with a sudden quell of panic, *she'll be next.* Growling, he lunged forward again, but Aaron had lured him into an icy trap of death, and had the high ground. Water splashed against Nathan's face and he blinked and felt fangs snag against his shoulder blade and push him further back into the waters. His legs began to quiver and tremble and he almost lost his balance for a moment. His muscles refused to obey his command – *patience,* he thought ironically, *I thought I had learned it, but Aaron is still the master.* He would wait until the young Alpha could barely stand and then lunge in for the kill.

His only chance would be to tackle him head on, and hope he could make his way up the shore and out of the cold grip of the lake. Nathan backed up a ways, and tipped his feet into the soft mud of the lake, looking for a good anchor-hold. He closed his eyes for half a second, visualizing the movement of his body sailing through the air, and then sprung into action.

Drops of water showered into the air as he charged at Aaron, but once again, his uncle was ready. Nathan felt more teeth wrench into his paw as he emerged from the water. He was so relieved to be free of the lake that he didn't see Aaron bring his body around like a viper and slam the whole weight of it down on his head. Nathan grunted and tasted a metallic edge slice across his tongue and then the mineral scent of the beach impact against his jaw. The world flickered, like someone playing with a light switch, and he tried to look up through the disorientation.

Aaron was almost laughing, a maniacal cackle that was unnervingly human but mixed with the hacking complexion of a dog choking on a bone. Nathan tried to stand up again, but his legs didn't belong to him, all of his muscles severed from their connection to his brain. *Can't move*, he moaned in the back of his consciousness, and his eyes closed against his will.

He waited.

And when Aaron's fangs didn't pierce his jugular, and he could still hear the lap of the creek and the passage of wind through the branches of hemlock, the distant scream of a hawk far above the mountain basin lost in its own orbit, he knew that he was still alive. His hind leg twitched, and he tried to stand up, only to be rewarded with another taste of mud as he collapsed.

Up the bank Aaron was cowering, his ears flat against the back of his head, and his muzzle stretched into a snarl. He was staring up at another animal – a beautiful dire wolf with a long flowing dark pelt, though not quite as dark as Nathan's. When the sun picked up off the lake and the reflections caught against it, a sudden flash of red would illuminate, like the darting body of a flame in the middle of the night. She stood almost as tall as the white dire wolf, but there was courage in her stance that was unmistakable.

Nika. He had to admit he knew next to nothing about his transgenic gene, or the sort of effects that it would have on humans, aside from what they'd already observed with her remarkable healing factor. But even among shifters, the ability to blend into their wolf-forms was something that didn't come until later on in life at the end of puberty, and only after they'd been able to meditate fully on the other presence in their mind. To think that after two days she had managed to fully integrate her wolf form was impossible. And yet, here she was, looming above his uncle, and her yellow-green eyes held no conflict in them. *She's made peace with her animal side already*, he thought with a mixture of pride and awe and fear.

Aaron growled again, snapping his teeth with the same chaotic pattern, as if he were battling not only Nika but also a deluge of imagined specters floating before his eyes. His leg was splayed out behind at a gross angle and had started to bleed again, and his white fur mopped it up and let it drip onto the grass beneath him. How he was still able to stand, Nathan had no idea, but he knew now he was at his most dangerous, especially if he smelled his own death approaching.

He opened his mouth to say something but only a whimper emanated from his lips.

Collecting whatever strength he had left, Aaron pushed forward with a gnashing of teeth. Nika met him head on, easily avoiding his attack, and sped forward, opening a gap in his defenses. It was anticlimactic and sudden – her mouth reached down on the side of his neck and squeezed, and there was a squeak of fangs incising inward. It was a perfect parody of Aaron's previous attack on her when she was a human, except this time, there was no joy in Nika's eyes.

Aaron buckled, pawing the air uselessly for a moment, and then went limp as her fangs severed his spinal column. He plummeted to the ground and his hind leg made a last spasm. Near the lake, Nathan had returned to his human form and sauntered, shivering, up the bank. He put his hand against Nika, feeling the softness of her fur tickle his palm, and rubbed the top of her muzzle. She purred and closed her eyes in deference.

At their feet, Aaron too was now shrinking into his own human form, and white hair fell off him like snow. His wrinkled pale body seemed such a pitiful alternative to the wolf he had once been, and he gurgled. In human form, the shotgun blast on his leg was purple and hemorrhaged, and there were numerous cuts on his body, masked with blood both wet and dry. He gurgled, his hands clawing the dirt, and looked up at his nephew.

Nathan stooped and held the old wolf's hand. "Hello uncle," he whispered.

"Young pup," he smiled, "I was just having a dream about you. You and Clara, oh, she was such a tenacious one in her youth – still is, I suppose. Such a pleasant dream."

"Tell me about it," he said, watching a dark red pool widen under him.

"We were… I don't know where we were. Somewhere on the prairies, because the sky was huge above us, and there was a big storm, but so far off we didn't have to worry. And there were horses. You know, I always liked horses, even though they hate our kind. Something… something about us, they can tell we're predators. But still, they're such beautiful creatures.

"You and Clara were spinning in a circle, laughing. Oh, and then Dean and Flores were there too. Ah, Flores, what a daughter. Her mother's beauty, and my brains – where is she, Nathan? Where's Flores?"

He was starting to lose coherence, and Nathan clenched his jaw. "She just stepped out. She'll be back any moment now. You'll see her soon," he muttered.

"Ah, good. Good. I have so many things to say to her… so many," he said, and his eyes closed.

Silence settled on all three of them, becoming another element among the water and stone and high alpine air, a nearly solid substance that cemented itself and pressed down with a private gravity. Behind him, Nika returned to her human shape as well and stood naked with the wind whipping at her hair, and put her hand on the back of Nathan's neck.

"I had no choice," she said.

He stood up and hugged her, pulling her against his chest, her breasts flattening against his skin, and let himself cry freely into her neck for long moments. "Thank you," he replied, and she wondered *for what*, then realized she had taken a burden from him, something unspeakably heavy. Had he been the one to put Aaron out of his misery, Nika wondered if he could have lived with it – *if this is the price, I pay it willingly,* she thought, and returned his embrace.

"We should do something… about his body," she replied.

He nodded. "We'll bury him here. He wouldn't have wanted some ornate, complex funeral, it's better this way. When we return, we'll say that he died of his wounds."

"You're worried about Dean," she said.

"Aye, but not just him. This is a stain on all shifters. And while we may pity Aaron for not being able to find peace in an era of human and shifter co-existence, we shall not dismiss him. He was a strong Alpha, and led the Pack through many struggles."

"He caused the destruction of a village… of his own daughter," she reminded tersely.

Nathan's reply was equally acidic. "Humans and shifters aren't so different," he explained, "the Pack will be shaken by Aaron's death for years. They need to believe in hope, they need to believe their leaders are wise and kind and have their best interests in mind. Maybe it's a lie, Nika, but Aaron died as one of us, a true shifter. That's how history will remember him."

"Wolves deserve wolves," she murmured, and it was the last time she would every repeat it.

*

"I'll take the cheesecake," Clara said, handing the leather-bound menu back to the waiter at their table, and poured another glass of wine. Across the table, Nika and Nathan were equally pensive as they lingered over the remains of their dinner. Beside her, Dean was fiddling with a piece of napkin.

The observation café in the Calgary Tower spun at a barely discernible rate, and now their table was facing west again, as if trying to follow the sun on its slow decline toward the Rocky Mountains. Under the table, Nathan reached for Nika's hand, and she took it gratefully. "You should watch your figure, sister," he said, "I know you need a lot of calories in order to compensate for being in wolf form for so long but don't you think you're overdoing it?"

She stuck her tongue out at him and sipped at her wine. "I think I've deserved it. If anything, I have a new appreciation for the finer things in life and I have no intention of depriving myself of them. Drink up, little brother," she said with mock seriousness, and refilled his glass. He winced, holding the purple liquid level to his eyes.

“Clara’s right,” Nika urged, nudging his shoulder with a smile. They were all tip-toeing around the same issue, but none of them had developed the courage to confront Clara about it. Dean dropped his napkin and sniffed loudly.

“What did the other packs decide?” he asked in a low treble.

Clara’s cheesecake came and she sliced a piece of it and closed her eyes, enjoying the sumptuous texture before she finally set her fork down and replied. “They had a hard time believing everything, but with our testimony, and with Corin’s help, they have decided to try and bury Aaron’s association to this whole mess,” but there was little in the way of consolation in her voice. “It will be blamed, officially, on the raiders – both Aaron and Flores are being considered heroes who died trying to protect the Pack.”

Dean’s fists clenched on top of the tablecloth. “And that’s it?”

Clara put a hand on his shoulder. “It’s better this way, Dean. I know you probably hate Aaron, but the other packs want to save face. They’ve also accepted Nathan as the Alpha; basically, they want things to go back to normal as soon as possible.”

“At least Flores is at peace,” Dean said with a hopeful rise in intonation

“She is,” Nathan said.

“What about… me?” Nika asked timidly, “I can’t imagine the sudden appearance of a new shifter in the Pack will simply go off without a hitch. How are they going to explain me?” A few tables around them suddenly looked in their direction and she lowered her head and tried to hide her face. Getting used to being a shifter, and keeping it a secret, was going to take some practice. *And how the hell do I break it to James*, she wondered.

This was news Clara didn’t mind sharing, and her face brightened. “Another deception, I’m afraid,” she said, “basically, you’ve always been a shifter. But the fact you were able to help out the Pack so much with this issue has given you some credit, as far as I’m concerned, and I’d like to see anyone disagree with me, you’re family.”

She nodded, her fingers tightened around Nathan’s. Still, she felt her throat tighten, and looked across the table at Dean. She and Nathan had told Clara about what had really happened in the final moments when Aaron had died, but they all decided to keep it a secret from Dean – it would have been hard enough for Dean if he’d been responsible for his own father’s death.

“What are you going to do now, Dean?” Nika asked, trying to change the subject.

He looked up at her and his beady eyes were more alive, as if the possibilities were endless, and he had only now perceived them flowing outward like a river entering the ocean. “I don’t know. I think… I think

I'll return to Corin's village. I made friends there and they still need a lot of help with rebuilding. I think I've grown tired of the city."

"That sounds nice," Clara nodded and ate another slice of her cheesecake.

"Yeah," Dean cracked a smile, "do you think Flores would be proud of me?"

"Definitely," she said.

"And what about you?" Nathan asked her, "Now that I'm Alpha, that puts you in a position of having to watch my back to make sure I don't make a fool of myself. Do you think you're really up to it?" They both shared a laugh and Clara scratched her eyebrow.

"I've been watching your back your whole life, idiot," she finished off her wine, "what makes you think I'd ever stop now?"

Afterward, after Clara and Dean headed back to the Den, Nika and Nathan pulled over next to the park where she had been attacked so many days ago, and she stepped off his bike. They walked hand in hand over the dim-lit paths, and veered off on a darkened side trail, but even in human form, their lupine affinity meant they could see just as well as if it were day.

On an empty bench, they both sat down, listening to the idle hum of the city. "Can you handle it?" he asked her suddenly, and she turned, not understanding. "The burden of the secret. It shouldn't have been you to kill Aaron and now you have to live with that decision. I can't help but feel it's my fault."

She shook her head, pulling the hem of her skirt over her bare legs. "I thought about it a lot, actually. What I'd be willing to sacrifice, if it meant saving someone or protecting someone I love," she said sagely, "and I decided I'd be able to endure a lot. Keeping a secret is nothing, compared to what else I've been through. And I still have you."

Nathan smiled and touched her thigh, moving his hand up under her skirt and she felt desire prickle at her senses again. "Always," he said.

For a moment, Nika felt self-conscious as she looked up and down the dark path, but there wasn't any sign of anyone, and the thrill of indulging in her own animal passions in such a public space was thrilling. More than that, it was like Clara said, that they had all earned the right to enjoy life. *And from now on Nathan is my life*, she resolved, leaning back as he moved his hand higher and his fingers brushed against her pubis.

"Stand up," he whispered, pulling a lock of hair around her neck, and she obeyed, not knowing what he had in mind until he gently turned around and braced his hands on her hips.

"I've never done it in a park before," she said over her shoulder, leaning forward until her hands clenched on the back of the bench. There was a reticence in her voice, which was alleviated by Nathan kissing her back and her shoulder.

His fingers moved, hiking up her skirt, and gently pulling down her panties. She gasped again, feeling the crisp air tingle up her thighs, and opened her legs wider. Even touching her for just an instant through the material, he had managed to arouse her, and she reached down and slid her middle finger against her vulva, urging herself wetter. Nathan pulled his zipper down and she heard the rustling of jeans as he pulled them to his ankles and moved forward, moving his hands up over her breasts.

"Do it," she said, and moaned as he pushed himself into her.

The wet slurp of his entrance caused her to jerk forward, and her hands clutched tighter against the cold steel of the bench as she arched her back and pushed her buttocks out. Nathan sighed and ground himself into her, squeezing the supple roundness of both cheeks. He thumped against her harder, coming to a full erection inside her vagina, and she croaked and bent forward.

His hands came off her breasts and over her hips again as he wound them toward her groin. She stood up, stroking the back of his head as she bent bow-like with his movements. His fingers moved closer, combing over the triangular ridge of her pubic region and through the stiff straight bristles until he touched her clitoris.

"Unh!" she said, straightening her back, and felt a wave of desire ripple through her whole body, "uh, careful, or I'll come right here."

"I want you to come," he teased.

"No," she murmured, "together… come with me."

He pushed his hand lower, avoiding her clitoris but sliding his fingers against the wet folds of her labia where his own penis plunged in and out of her, lubricated with both of their innate need to exhaust themselves. Behind her, Nathan groaned and pulled out of her, and her skirt fell, sliding against the damp tip of his penis. He sat back down on the bench and she stooped over him, sitting down on his lap with her back toward him.

He spread her legs wider and began to rub her sex in vigorous strokes as he re-entered her. She leaned back against him, giving into the moment, and satisfied to let him explore her own body as his temple, his canvas, as an extension of his own body. Sweat pooled off her inner thighs, and she started to moan in panicky animal sounds, gritting her teeth and licking her lips.

Nathan thrust harder as she fell against his chest and one his hands came up from the sticky mess of her pubis to fondle her breasts through her blouse. He felt her nipples harden against the fabric as he fucked her with the unrelenting passion of a wolf, and both of them growled at one another as their communal climax bubbled to the surface.

“It’s coming,” he murmured into her shoulder.

“Yes!” she exclaimed, opening her legs wider. His fingers spread out as he cupped her groin, and the dark skin of her inner thighs quivered for an instance as the orgasm came on like a blinding flash in the corner of her mind. “Yes, hold me,” she squirmed.

His hand moved up and he planted his palm firmly against the space between her pubis and navel as her stomach undulated with muscular tension and she let out a muffled scream. Nathan came at the same time and grunted as he pulled out, his stiff member snapping to attention like elastic, and rubbed against the red bead of her inflamed clitoris.

“God, Nathan!” she said, as a second orgasm overlaid on top of the first, and she reached down and grabbed his penis as it jetted its seed into the air and across the naked landscape of her belly, where it drooled down into the black quills of her pubic hair.

He held her again as she rocked, familiar enough now with her rhythms to know how to keep her from hurting herself as she succumbed to her climax. When she finally took in a deep breath and relaxed against him, both were drained and caught in the ecstatic doldrums of endorphins. She stood shakily and pulled her panties back up under her skirt and Nathan zipped his pants again, and the two of them walked several feet onto the cut lawn and laid down on their backs.

Nika raised her hand toward the sky, opening her fingers against the sky as she tried to invent her own constellations out of the stars. It had always been difficult to make out the Milky Way because of the light pollution in Calgary, but tonight it was particularly clear, as if the cosmos itself had turned up its brightness in order to punch through the orange bath of city iridescence.

Nathan's own rough hand came up next to hers, splayed outward. "Are you still afraid?" she asked, remembering his speech about how fear had its uses.

"No," he admitted, "I don't feel the need to be afraid anymore."

"Why not?"

He shrugged, not sure how to answer. "I don't know," he said, "for so long I've relied on it to keep me awake, to keep me astute, never questioned it, or the fact that a small amount of fear was the one thing keeping me alive. But now, I guess I just found something else to feel, something stronger than fear."

His fingers spread between her own and held them pinned against the Big Dipper, which forever circled around the axis of the North Star. "And what's that?" she asked.

"Silly girl," he murmured, ***"I love you."***

THE END

Message From The Author:

Thanks so much for reading all the way to the end, I really hope you enjoyed it. If you did I would love it if you could leave me a rating. This helps other people find my books :)

By the way, you can check out and see ALL my other shifter releases by taking a look at ***my Amazon page here!***

*

*

Get Yourself a FREE Bestselling Paranormal Romance Book!

Join the "**Simply Shifters**" Mailing list today and gain access to an exclusive **FREE** classic Paranormal Shifter Romance book by one of our bestselling authors along with many others more to come. You will also be kept up to date on the best book deals in the future on the hottest new Paranormal Romances. We are the HOME of Paranormal Romance after all!

*** Get FREE Shifter Romance Books For Your Kindle & Other Cool giveaways**

*** Discover Exclusive Deals & Discounts Before Anyone Else!**

*** Be The FIRST To Know about Hot New Releases From Your Favorite Authors**

Click The Link Below To Access Get All This Now!

SimplyShifters.com

Already subscribed?
OK, *Turn The Page!*

ALSO BY JASMINE WHITE....

FATED TO THE ALPHA

Evelyn has a dark secret. A secret so dark, that if her pack found out she could be sentenced to death.

However, now it could be time for the secret to come out.

Evelyn has been slated to marry Leon, the Alpha of her pack. Only she feels she can't. That is because she is love with someone else.

That someone else, is Jeremy, a wolf from a most-hated rival pack. The feud between the packs is almost at breaking point and this could be the incident that pushes everything over the edge.

Jeremy can not stand by and watch the woman he loves be married off to the Alpha. He knows he has to rescue his woman, even if he has to risk his life and face certain death to do so....

This is a gripping story of star crossed lovers, feuding shifters and furry heroes

START READING NOW AT THE BELOW LINK!

Amazon.com >
http://www.amazon.com/dp/B00XLS37IK

Amazon UK >
http://www.amazon.co.uk/dp/B00XLS37IK

Amazon Australia >
http://www.amazon.com.au/dp/B00XLS37IK

Amazon Canada >
http://www.amazon.ca/dp/B00XLS37IK